One Thousand
& One

Kari Hukkila

One Thousand
& One

Translated from the Finnish
by David Hackston

Contra Mundum Press   New York · London · Melbourne

One Thousand & One
© 2023 David Hackston;
Kari Hukkila, *Tuhat ja yksi*
© 2016 Kari Hukkila.
Published originally in Finnish
by Teos Publishers. Published
by agreement with Helsinki
Literary Agency.

First Contra Mundum Press
edition 2023.

Library of Congress
Cataloguing-in-Publication
Data

Hukkila, Kari, 1955
One Thousand and One /
Kari Hukkila

—1st Contra Mundum Press
Edition

280 pp., 5×8 in.

ISBN 9781940625621

 I. Hukkila, Kari.
 II. Title.
 III. Hackston, David.
 IV. Translator.

2023945181

This work has been published with the financial
assistance of FILI – Finnish Literature Exchange.
Contra Mundum Press gratefully acknowledges
the financial assistance of FILI – Finnish
Literature Exchange.

TABLE OF CONTENTS

*This translation is dedicated
to the memory of Tarja Roinila (1964 – 2020)
translator, colleague, friend
gone too soon*

The Duck-Rabbit
Ludwig Wittgenstein, Philosophical Investigations

ON THE CUSP OF A NOVEL

Since April, it had been clear that on Thursday, June 17, I would drive from Helsinki to Uukuniemi on the eastern border, where I would focus on work that had been weighing on my shoulders all spring because it had to do with a falling out with some members of my family. *I'm going to the countryside, there's nothing else for it, I'll be there over Midsummer, four or five weeks,* I'd said to a good friend who called from Rome and reminded me of the promise I'd made to visit him at Midsummer. When I arrived at the cabin on Thursday at around midnight, even from a distance I could see that two tall birch trees from the neighbor's property had fallen across the fence and come crashing down over the veranda of my small Swiss-style log cabin, their boughs and wrist-thick branches reached many meters into the air, but the structure beneath them looked intact, though the trees had fallen right across the veranda and become wedged in front of the door.

I tried to clear a path to the door, it was futile, and an hour later I decided to sleep on the bed in the sauna changing room, but sleep would not come. I was supposed to start work at ten o'clock tomorrow (June 18), next Friday (Midsummer's Eve, June 25) I was due to go over my notes, while on the following Friday (July 2) my work would be half-done, giving me some

kind of observation post from which to look out over
the whole. I'd decided not to let anything destabilize
my schedule and the stages of my work, and now I
was tossing and turning on my temporary bed, the
birches would be sorted out eventually, I wouldn't get
started on my work, and once I eventually managed
to fall asleep at around 4 A.M., a loud cuckoo started
making a racket in the bough of the tree above me as
though marking the hour and the half hour. In the
morning, the situation with the birches looked every bit as desperate as it had the previous night. *You
wouldn't believe what it looks like here, two enormous
birches, just when I was supposed to start work*, I told
Mara when he called later that afternoon, I knew
he would use the opportunity to invite me to Rome
again. *You can chop your logs later*, he said the way he
always said I'd be able to postpone my Wittgenstein
many times yet, and he was right. As a young man
he had chopped his own Wittgenstein logs, at barely
twenty years of age he was on course to become the
new rising star of the internationally acclaimed Finnish Wittgenstein school, in this respect he was on the
[1, 2] same pathway as von Wright or Hintikka, who had

1   Finland-Swedish philosopher Georg Henrik von Wright (1916–
    2003), affectionately known throughout the novel as Jori
    Henrik & a close friend & colleague of Ludwig Wittgenstein.
    [All notes have been added during the translation process.]

2   Finnish philosopher Jaakko Hintikka (1929–2015).

chopped their Wittgenstein logs better than anyone else, but to everyone's dismay Mara had decided to quit philosophy, for good, as he told everybody. *Two tall birches have toppled over, each weighing over a ton,* I told him. There's a small, abandoned cabin on the neighbor's property that nobody has visited for at least twenty years, I said in answer to Mara's question, there were a dozen or so fallen trees on the neighboring plot, large birches lying one on top of the other. I ended the phone call abruptly, got to go, *boondocks*, Friday, weekend about to start, I had to travel fifteen kilometers, an old librarian acquaintance will know what to do, I told Mara as I walked around the cabin, and though the building itself didn't seem to have sustained any damage, I was plagued by the sense of a twist of fate, the gust of wind that felled those birches had also struck my work, which I'd been planning since April.

The confrontation with my relatives had started at the end of March when, in a moment of thoughtlessness, I'd decided to attend one of their *anniversary dinners* at the restaurant on Uunisaari, which had been booked for the occasion. [3]

The argument started almost out of the blue. They didn't like *that book of mine*, as they called it.

3 An island a short boat crossing from the shores of Kaivopuisto.

4

A few months previously, I'd noticed that my brother, nine years my junior, was active on a number of *anti-immigration nonsense forums*, as I told him in due course, adding that all that nonsense reminded me of a collective drunken euphoria with its illusory sense of community and that *you can't sort people like cattle*, as I also told him. The sense of such forums as a public pastime made me shudder, they reminded me of the collapse of my family bonds and otherwise elicited *adverse reactions*, yet only a moment earlier, as I'd walked from the shores of Kaivopuisto[4] across the winter bridge to Uunisaari, I hadn't suspected a thing... The damp, Scandinavian fog, the smell of the sea and last year's straggly grass, from the bridge I could barely see the island's red-brick buildings and dark, imposing tree trunks. At the restaurant door, I turned back toward the patio, where a group of smokers, my brother included, was puffing away, unaware that the same ideological front that at that very moment in spring 2010 divided not only Finland but the whole of Europe from Athens to Budapest and all the way to Stockholm would moments later divide this group of smokers too. I said something about the cabin in Uukuniemi. *When you go to the countryside, just look around a bit*, my brother said, and though he never actually visited

4 One of the oldest & most well-known parks in central Helsinki, Finland.

the countryside himself he meant that life out in the boondocks was somehow *real*, at least compared to *that book of mine*. Before long someone was holding forth about *values* and *welfare* and goodness knows what... Nothing but *sorting words* and *barbed-wire words*, Mara and I agreed on the phone the following day, these are exactly the people who could do with a little dose of Wittgenstein and Björling, said   5 Mara, mentioning both his ideal philosopher and his ideal poet, the way he did in almost any interaction.

Anybody else can be kept at arm's length, but not a brother.

He didn't educate himself, didn't travel, didn't care about behavioral niceties, I liked that, he didn't shake hands, didn't engage in inane small talk; when we were young, he used to greet me by gently pressing a fist against my chest, but no longer. A few years earlier, he had reluctantly moved to Turku for work, and since then we've been in contact only rarely. Once the group of smokers at Uunisaari moved indoors, we were all ushered toward the same corner of the table, and the confrontation that had started outside only worsened. No matter what I said, my brother

5 Finland-Swedish poet Gunnar Björling (1887–1960) was described by Marjorie Perloff as "a milestone in the annals of experimental poetics produced in our century." He lived almost his entire life on the outskirts of Kaivopuisto, Helsinki.

retorted with a jeering *big deal*, and an older relative sitting nearby looked at me silently, a malice in his eyes, only the corner of his mouth twitching beneath his beard each time my brother scoffed another *big deal*.

Later that evening, once I'd left Uunisaari, I started writing notes, trying to work out where exactly their drunken euphoria had come from, and though these notes wouldn't necessarily tell me about my brother, they would tell me about what happens within us. In the days that followed, I tried to latch on to those small states of exception creeping closer, one tree at a time, and the reality where, in matters both large and small, we seek to sort people. I was writing these notes for myself, my brother would never read them, but everything I wrote I tried to formulate as a rebuttal of his *big deal*, I would push back against the jeering until I flattened his barbed-wire fence, but after trying for a few days I still felt powerless in the face of that thought-terminating jeer (the older relative even sent me a two-line email renouncing his family ties to me). Eventually, I turned to the works of Gustaw Herling, the Polish writer who was sent to the gulag at the age of twenty and who published one of the earliest first-hand depictions of life at the Soviet labor camps. Later, while living in Naples, Herling turned his gulag-weary eyes to earthquakes and other local catastrophes and saw in them the patterns he had witnessed in the camps.

My thoughts of barbed wire, however, were closer to home. As I was approaching Uukuniemi the previous night I'd seen the familiar 15 kg rolls of barbed wire and electric fencing stacked by the wall at the village store in Niukkala, the rolls of wire had appeared there the previous summer when a local farmer had bought his first bison. A year ago, the bison grazing in the vast green fallow fields had recalled the adventure books of my childhood, Karl May, Winnetou and Old Shatterhand, but now the barbed wire reminded me of Herling and my brother.

Out in the countryside, I would write about Herling and about *us*, or so I'd planned. I would work from morning until late in the evening. I would have only short pauses, sit on the wooden jetty and feed the ducks that turned up for that very purpose at the same time every afternoon, I would heat up the sauna, start every day with a dip in the lake regardless of the weather, and live as simply as possible. Trips to the village store were long, Niukkala was 15 km away, and the larger supermarket in Kesälahti a full 33 km. The rest of my time I would spend at my desk with my 0.5mm-nib felt-tip pen from Muji, making notes and sketching pathways to help me grasp not only my brother but my thoughts about the barbed wire too, which reminded me of the English title of Herling's book, *A World Apart*, and walking along these pathways by my side, I imagined my brother as a traveling companion. I'd even planned that, one hot day, I would take the boat and head almost all the way to the border, out to the island of Suitsa where there is a forest owned by the Stora Enso Company, a small sandy beach and an unlocked cabin, nothing but a small shack made of faded planks that was once used by loggers back in the 1970s, only a ten-minute walk from the former border station. From the shack you could see the old observation post rising up above the trees. It too had been abandoned; nowadays the Border Guard's Koala helicopter flew north along the border twice a week, heading directly across the open lake, where a row of yellow poles marked the border. In the summer, the smoke from forest fires on the opposite shore hung in the air, the opposite shore being Russia, though there were no people or signs of habitation in sight. Since April, this forest had meant only one thing to me. These were Herling's forests. He had felled giant pine trees at the Yertsevo labor camp, only 500 km to the east, in essentially the exact same forest, therefore. During the winter, the prisoners cut down the surrounding forest in snow a meter and a half deep, and in his book about the gulag I learnt almost right away that of all the nationalities represented at the camp, the Finns were the most experienced when it came to forestry. Naturally, the suffering Herling endured at the camp is of a different magnitude from what most people experience, but I imagined that in such extreme and exceptional circumstances as those into which Herling was forced, one might be able to see something about ordinary everyday life, perhaps even about the most private of catastrophes, and if only I could penetrate Herling's forests, they would no longer tell only the story of his life or, indeed, his times. They would also tell us something about the reality of 2010.

And right now I should be sitting at my desk, huddled away under those birches... I was driving back along the road that only twelve hours earlier I'd driven in the opposite direction. The fallen birches were like two jeers weighing a ton each, *big deal*, massive, mighty allies of my relatives and my brother, their boughs rotten, and the crown of every birch still standing was cracked, they would all soon topple over, I thought. That morning, the librarian and I had arranged that I could arrive shortly before the branch closed. On the left-hand side of the road, I caught sporadic flashes of yellow tape tied around the tree trunks, the border zone, the dust tracks ending in signs with a red hand raised to stop wanderers, *Gränszon, Grenzzone, Frontier Zone, Пограничная зона...* I tried to banish the idea of a twist of fate that had been bothering me, but I only forgot about it when I met the librarian, who had already got things moving, she had called the municipal council and several land-surveyance offices that had been closed down years ago until she finally got lucky and found some details relating to the neighboring plot. The owner, an elderly lady, answered the phone in a hushed, sing-song voice, terribly friendly, though she seemed a bit demented, and her words reminded me of the smokers' notions of Finland earlier in the spring… *the birches, the birches, oh I remember them well, every last one of them, the birches in the garden, that's right, they're so soothing, I'm sure we brought them with us from Karelia, that's how the old song goes, isn't it, how did it go again, the birches, ah yes, the birches in the garden, they're so pretty, how are they keeping*, eventually she gave us permission to clear them and a moment later the only logger in the area promised to pop by later that evening on his way between two work sites to inspect the damage.

I stayed there talking to the librarian once the library had closed for the day. Mailis — as I'd called her since long before I ever knew her surname — is a great conversationalist, always looking out for new authors to read. Originally an Uukuniemi local, she had left Helsinki and moved back here at the age of forty, making her the only person I know to have done so. I told her that earlier in the winter I'd promised to visit Mara in Rome but had been forced to postpone my departure. The librarian was well aware who Mara was and often asked how he was doing, though she didn't know him personally. She always referred to Mara by his real name, and sometimes even used his surname too. In fact, Mara would enjoy life here far better than he did where he was now, I told her, the only reason he was in Rome was because a university acquaintance had offered to rent him an apartment. Wittgenstein's cabin, situated in the village of Skjolden at the far end of Sognefjord in Norway, was about the best thing Mara could imagine, I said. I'd once tried to invite him to Uukuniemi by mentioning, half in jest, that the cabin here was rather similar to the Skjolden cabin, which was just over 70 m² in size, both had a small study, a sleeping area, a living space with a kitchen in the corner, both used water from the lake, the Skjolden cabin was thirty meters from the shore and at least thirty meters above water level, whereas at Uukuniemi the shore was at most five meters away and no more than five above the water, most important was that both places were far away from other people, *in der Einsamkeit*, as Wittgenstein said, *out in the loneliness*, as Mara rendered it in inimitable Finland-Swedish style. 6

6 Around 5% of the Finnish population speak Swedish as their native language. Mara is one such person. This demographic has many names, but throughout this translation they are referred to as Finland-Swedes.

Mara had always thrived in the simplest, most ascetic conditions possible, I told Mailis. He even referred to philosophy as *gutting*. He *gutted* things and sometimes even *sorted* things, but only thoughts. He wasn't one of those thinkers constantly retreating to his ivory tower, as people always say of philosophers. He avoided academia, though at one time he and a group of academics used to visit the prime minister's summer residence, hobnobbing with politicians who were *rolling up their sleeves*, as they put it, *steadying the ship*, by which they meant the state. The politicians were quick to read the room and they spoke in assertive, confidence-inspiring terms, while Mara's entourage was marked by a certain *performative uncertainty*, a common mannerism in academic circles. Upon meeting these men at the prime minister's residence, it was clear they were all perfectly at home in the forest, hunting, accustomed to moving in a hunting chain. They engaged in *sham hunting* and *sham fishing*, while professional snipers behind them did the real work, whereas the academics engaged in *sham thinking*, which when Mara said it sounded like some kind of comedic hunting convoy and recalled the diplomatic visits across the Soviet border of bygone decades, which Mara heard so much about at the prime minister's residence, *and they visited these same tracts*, Mailis chuckled.

That evening, once I'd returned to the cabin from the grocery store in Kesälahti, I picked up Herling and started reading. Barely a few minutes later, I heard a tractor rattling into the yard. The logger jumped down from the cab in his overalls, and when we reached the fallen birches, he said this wasn't going to be a *fifteen-minute job*, as if to demonstrate this he kicked the nearest tree trunk and added *it'll have to be after Midsummer.* He took his chainsaw and cut back enough of the branches to allow me at least to open the front door a little. That evening, I cleared the shards of glass from the floor and carefully examined the roof; I couldn't see any damage. Still, I thought it wise to continue sleeping in the sauna changing room. Around ten o'clock that evening, Mara called again and asked what had happened with the birches. I told him I hadn't even started on my work, as I'd planned. He'd had a little *mishap* too, he used this very word, *that's right, here, an illegal.* I asked what kind of mishap that was, but he seemed reluctant to talk about it. *Stumbled upon him, by chance, only known him a day or two, I'll tell you later*, he didn't want to talk about it *right this minute* and gave a staid snigger, the way Finland-Swedes do when it's something serious. They are always so *behaved*, unlike us Finnish speakers, I thought. Even Mara knew how to *behave*, it came naturally to him, as it did to all Finland-Swedes.

The Kontula apartment's sold, he said, deftly changing the subject. I knew that his mother had died quite recently and he had inherited his childhood home. *It went for a song,* he said, *first you pay through the nose for your past, then you're so keen to see the back of it that you'll sell to the lowest bidder.* Eventually, he asked yet again when I was planning to visit him. *It's been a year since we had a walk together.* When Mara lived in Helsinki, he used to phone me and suggest we go for a walk, out of politeness he would always suggest we meet in Kaivopuisto, though we never went for a walk anywhere else. Kaivopuisto had everything he needed to *sort* his thoughts, Björling's former residence on Itäinen puistokatu, a room on the ground floor of a building originally intended as a public sauna, and at the other end of the route von Wright's house on Laivurinkatu. Mara called several times over the following days. *The trees can wait*, and Naples was Herling's landscape too, he said when I told him about the Herling project that I wanted to carry out in this very forest. When a friendship is long enough, you do what the birds and the herrings do, you turn when your neighbor turns, that's how naturalists explain the unfathomable formations of birds and shoals of fish, I said to Mailis when I told her I'd decided to join Mara after all and return to Uukuniemi once I got back. The following Friday, only a week after Mara's first phone call, I was sitting on the morning Finnair flight from Helsinki to Rome, gazing out of the window. Unimaginably tall cloud-statues rose up like solitary giants from the undulating cumulus blanket beneath, light glistering along their edges. I opened the Blue Wings in-flight magazine and soon found Herling's Yertsevo on the map, Uukuniemi didn't look very far away at all, and both were at approximately the same latitude as Wittgenstein's Skjolden in Norway. Once we landed, the heat struck me in the face. It was over 30°C, my steps slowed by half. Before six o'clock, I was strolling along the Campo dei Fiori, where we had agreed to meet in front of Ristorante Carbonara. I arrived early and gawked around in different directions to see whether Mara might have arrived early too, but there were so many tourists thronging around me that I retreated next to a row of potted shrubs, standing a meter and a half tall, lining the terrace outside the restaurant. I peered between two of them and watched the waiters. There weren't any customers sitting at the tables outside; it wasn't quite dinner-time yet. There were two waiters, each leaning into his own little alcove. Both were wearing black trousers, an orange shirt, a dark-brown apron, each had a pen in his breast pocket and a cloth over his forearm. Some customers appeared, a couple, and all three of us noticed them at once. The younger waiter waved his cloth as if to banish the stuffy air, wiped his brow with it, then both waiters began walking toward the couple at precisely the same moment, both took out their pens, as if each had got the idea from the other. One of them started taking the couple's order, leaving the other to whack an empty chair next to him with his folded cloth. I glanced at the time, five to six, then looked around for Mara, and saw him in the distance almost immediately.

I
ONE THOUSAND

There must be a thousand of those busts...
— Mara

I got you here after all, Mara's face lit up when he saw me, and I could almost hear a contented chuckle. I saw large sweat stains in his shirt armpits, either from heat or nerves; when he was younger, he even got nervous about meeting me. Before long, he was standing next to me cursing the crush of tourists in that impeccably polite way of his, he gently squeezed my arm, asked about the journey and how I was keeping, and mentioned his recent visit to Helsinki for his mother's funeral, it was only three weeks ago, I'd known about it but hadn't had the opportunity to meet him at the time. Helsinki felt entertaining, he said, who would have thought, under the circumstances. On the Friday, before the funeral, he had taken a walk along the shores at Kaivopuisto. One after another, all my old acquaintances walked past me, he said. There was something approaching relief about seeing all those people. *I survived my mother's funeral.* On his walk through Kaivopuisto he even bumped into some people who ought to have been here at Villa Lante, and all those with whom he had worked ^{7} on philosophy years ago, they've all left philosophy

7 A Renaissance palace designed by the architect Giulio Romano and nowadays owned by the Republic of Finland, Villa Lante al Gianicolo houses the Finnish Institute in Rome, which offers residencies and scholarships to Finnish artists and researchers.

now, he said. Hainari, another childhood friend from Kontula, was the first one he'd bumped into. Hainari had left philosophy long before him, and before so-and-so, and so-and-so. Nowadays he studied Russian every day in order to read Tolstoy and Dostoyevsky in the original. Mara waved his hand as if to embody Hainari's affectations as he'd said that *thought has no place in the ways of the world anymore.* Yet again, I noticed how much Mara reminded me of Jeremy Irons, a joke we'd been telling about him for years. *At your own mother's funeral, you think nothing worse than this can ever happen*, he said. I've always had a difficult relationship with my brother, and since I turned my back on philosophy he's been giving me an even wider berth, he didn't care about philosophy either, I'm sure he barely knew what it was, but at least he thought of it as some kind of *workplace*, whereas with my mother nothing ever worked, she couldn't stand anything I did, Mara explained, this time gesticulating toward his childhood home somewhere in the distance while the waiters at the Carbonara started almost aggressively ushering us to a table, they pulled out the chairs by their backrests and seemed wholly unpleasant. I already felt lonely at the funeral, said Mara, but at a moment like that you think nothing worse than this can ever happen,

8 An eastern suburb of Helsinki.

as though the funeral was the culmination of decades of family misery because now everything was over and nothing could ever be fixed again. On the flight home, the loneliness escalated into a mortal panic, he said, I leafed through Wittgenstein's *Tractatus* and his notebooks from 1914–1916, which I'd stuffed into my pocket as I cleared out the childhood crap from the Kontula apartment, but the same mortal panic poured forth from those pages too, and of course once Wittgenstein really got his work underway in Norway at the age of twenty-four, without any obvious reason he became convinced that he was going to die within two months, and from that point onward one always wonders whether he was committing suicide or doing something extraordinary and constructive. The longer the flight went on, the more visceral the feeling of loneliness became, and once I got back to the apartment here, it was impossible to remain inside; indoors the air was empty, dead, everything reminded me of the moment when I was *leaving* for the funeral. First I thought of going to Lante, there's always some function or other going on in the evenings, but I didn't go, he said. I met this Ethiopian, *you know*, he met my eyes in a way that meant *of course, a real rascal, that goes without saying.* He'd gone to the train station, had a coffee at one of the kiosks, watched the people placing their luggage on the floor and hugging one another goodbye.

He'd wandered off without any definitive destination and ended up in the area behind the station. That night, he ended up in bed with the Ethiopian, you know, at his apartment. I thought he was from southern Italy, said Mara, and it was only the following evening that he told me he's actually from Ethiopia, and when I asked what he was doing here he said, the same as the Italians in Ethiopia, nothing much. He asked what I'd been up to, nothing much either, I said, it's not like I was about to tell him my life story, and he laughed, *va be'*, the whole situation genuinely seemed to amuse him. He said he was glad to be here, and it was only then that he told me he was an illegal. He left my place on Tuesday morning but never came back, said Mara, and he left behind a small bag at the apartment, toiletries, deodorant, pretty much all his belongings, and it was only afterwards that I started thinking he doesn't have a place in the world *either*, he's excluded from the ways of the world too, just as I'd heard by the shores of Kaivopuisto that thought no longer had a place in the ways of world, and of course if you're an illegal it's all but impossible.

We walked away from the worst of the crowds. Mara said something in Swedish that I didn't understand but compensated with a revealing hand gesture. *It's ridiculous...* Well, the next day I was lying in bed, *and this really is ridiculous*, at first I hardly noticed it, it started itching, what's the word in Finnish…? Well, anyway, I got it from the Ethiopian, *what the hell is it in Finnish…*? No matter, the following day I had to boil all my clothes, all the bed linen, *by hand*, because the apartment doesn't have a washing machine. I had to boil *everything* several times, all my clothes, and rinse them and wring them dry. By the time I'd finished, my hands were covered in blisters and there was an unbearable heat wave going on too, and after my mother's death there were a few other things I needed to sort out, but the worst of it was that on laundry days like this you have time to think about your life many times over. *It's an infernal job*, all that rinsing and wringing, it had me wondering whether I ought to have moved back to Helsinki after all, but I'd already put the Kontula apartment on the market. Every day I wondered what it would be like to wander along the shore at Kaivopuisto right now, I've thought about it many times over the course of my life, and then on top of that to find myself in *this infernal sauna*, he said. When Mara was talking about the *sauna*, I was reminded of Herling, whom I'd been reading on the way here, Herling, the shaven heads, the scarred backs, the camp sauna they visited once every three weeks, and that's when they saw the effects of life in the camp, how much they had thinned, the steam measured their lives, what was left of it. *All this happened at once*, said Mara. I met the Ethiopian on the

Sunday, and only the day before I'd been in Helsinki at my mother's funeral and *from the funeral I went straight to Kontula, still in my suit*, I had to empty the apartment, my brother had already taken everything he was willing to take, everything with sentimental value. I hadn't been inside my parents' apartment very often over the years. *There in the top cupboard in my old bedroom were all the philosophy books from my youth. I sat in front of the window, in the room that had once been mine, I threw the books into black plastic sacks and carried them out to the dumpster,* and that was just the Saturday. I opened every book, looked through the bits I'd underlined, now and then I had to sit back and calm down and try to think of something else. When small farmsteads were foreclosed in the 1970s, everybody kicked up an almighty fuss; nowadays, when everything that requires even the slightest thought is foreclosed, there's no fuss at all. *Everything valuable is just thrown away,* he said. *Just as the farms were closed down, now thought is being closed down too.* I sat there in front of the window looking at those grey and blue paperbacks, and it occurred to me that these were the books with which I lost some of my mental immaturity... Mara shook his head and pointed to a sign a little further ahead with the familiar Guinness lyre. We walked into the pub, the air conditioning made me shiver, a string of Irish flags hung from the ceiling, he asked me if I remembered a stranger who'd once sat down at our table in a bar years ago. The stranger, a man from the back of beyond in Northern Karelia, disliked Helsinki, called it a dreary place, back home the landscape was so beautiful that, when you spent the night with a girl, the following morning you rushed up one of the old look-out towers to admire the panorama. He was already *shepherding* at the age of fifteen, he told us, hiking through the woods with a saxophone slung over his shoulder, but a few years later when the farms were foreclosed and the cows taken to the slaughterhouse, *every farm* had the same problem, and there at our table, in his Icelandic woolen sweater and with tankard in hand, he sighed the names of all the cows... *You always try to save the cow you lost your virginity with till last, but eventually you've got to slaughter that one too, and that's just terrible... That's how I felt about those books*, Mara chuckled.

You can't imagine how I cursed the Ethiopian once I was through with that damn sauna and finally got out for a walk. I cursed him but still couldn't get him out of my mind, said Mara, and I realized he'd just been waiting for the right moment to start talking about the Ethiopian again. *I cursed him to the lowest circle of laundry hell, but I still couldn't find him.* After the infernal sauna I wanted to get outdoors, but the city center was so full of tourists that I couldn't stroll around there, the Kontula apartment was on the market, and when the realtor called that afternoon after a viewing I couldn't hear a word she was saying in all the downtown hullabaloo. Meanwhile, the area along the riverside south of *centro storico* was as deserted as always… Of course, I know that wasn't the only reason I was down there by the embankment, but that night I'd got the impression that's where the Ethiopian would be hanging out, there were lots of illegals down there… Anyway, I cursed to myself and walked along the embankment, there's a track or more like a small pathway strewn with litter running through the reeds, sometimes there's a strip of asphalt and a few workmen's porta potties, though there's nobody doing any actual work there. In late summer, the path gets overgrown with reeds, but earlier in the season there's still enough room to walk along it.

Mara asked whether I knew the area along the river with the tall gasholder. I nodded, I knew the place he meant, only a few days later I passed it on the Line B subway. Through the carriage window, I caught a brief glimpse of some impressive, long since decommissioned industrial buildings and unfathomable steel constructions whose original function I no longer recognized. The steel arches, girders, and halls looked in turn like grain silos, observatories, and prison camps. Plants sprawled wild along the gables and ceilings of the abandoned buildings and were well on course to consume the buildings in their entirety. Mara explained that the industrial area was built in the 1920s. It used to house a gas facility, and the gasholder standing a full 90m tall was still operational. Only a few decades ago, the area had boasted a riverside wharf, a soap factory, an electricity company and a large market hall that was first opened to the public in 1922. One of the factory buildings produced optical equipment for the Italian air force and somewhere else there was a company that used to manufacture parachutes. An enormous abattoir was still in use through the 1950s, when farmers used to walk their cattle to the slaughter along the streets at night. He had heard that archaeologists had recently discovered an old bend in the Almone, which centuries ago used to run right under the market hall. *I was thinking about the Ethiopian*, he said, *I cursed him and cursed myself too, of course.* From what he said, I'd got the impression that the damn Ethiopian would be somewhere around here, a few kilometers on from the old industrial area.

Over the next two days, I walked several kilometers further along the riverbank, said Mara. The embankment was nothing but abandoned wasteland, and the further I walked the more abandoned it became. Reeds and undergrowth sprawled everywhere. A wooden, three-story pontoon structure looked like it had simply keeled over into the water and been abandoned. The path followed the riverbank, a steep embankment several meters tall rose up to the side, behind that was a dense wall of bushes and reeds three meters tall, and behind the tangled thicket a wire fence running for several kilometers separated the riverbank and one of the main thoroughfares through Ostiense. Further off among the bushes were shacks that the homeless had knocked together, and all around was a frightful amount of trash. I was in an unusual state of mind, said Mara, something inside me brought out a searing anger, and whenever I cursed, I glanced across to the other side of the river, where a pastoral idyll stood barely fifty meters away. There was a stable and what looked like some kind of enclosure where a rider geed his horse into motion and jumped again and again over an obstacle that I couldn't see. Behind the fence, a few horses craned their necks toward the ground. On the lawn, a woman threw a ball or a stick, and a dog ran off to fetch it. Behind the boughs of the trees stood a row of high-rise buildings from the 1960s, each with identical strip balconies. On the other side of the river, people lived a normal life; on this side, a sliver of overgrown wasteland stretched out in front of me, precisely the kind of wasteland you should avoid round here, but to do that I ought to have turned off toward the Ostiense highway several kilometers back, whereas if I walked any further along the riverbank, I would have to pass the shacks behind the bushes and the embankment.

On the third day, I sensed that something might happen with the apartment, I was irritated and resolved to walk past the shacks no matter what happened. There was a pungent whiff of smoke in the air. It wasn't coming from a campfire; someone somewhere was burning plastic, a terrible stench. The realtor called about Kontula, and with that the apartment was sold. I'd barely ended the call when I heard voices coming from behind the thicket, the homeless people were Romanian Roma, just as I'd assumed the day before, because just like the day before I was reminded of Wittgenstein, probably because his work with the later *Tractatus* reached its culmination in the borderlands between Romania and Ukraine during the First World War amid far greater destruction than all the crap and detritus lying along the riverbank. I continued walking, and a few of the Roma appeared on the embankment and watched me walk past, they said something, asked what I was doing there and told me it was *dangerous* to hang around places like this, and I was terrified, wondering what on earth I'd got myself into... *No, no, I didn't find the Ethiopian, and nothing happened*, Mara replied to my question as he stood up from his chair and headed to the bathroom.

I'd been listening to Mara's story with increasing concern. If you *stumble* into places that everyone else avoids like the plague, you'll soon find yourself in danger, and I told him so as he stood up from the table. He was looking for trouble, or something worse still. And just as he had said he was *offloading* everything onto the Ethiopian, that is, everything on his mind, I now *offloaded* everything I heard in Mara's speech onto his constant *stumbling*. For my part, this was a spontaneous reaction to what he had told me. I hadn't seen him for a year, and now I'd stumbled upon this little scenario, and the fact that he mentioned Wittgenstein and his experiences of the war only confirmed that Mara was looking for trouble, or something worse still, Wittgenstein was almost the worst thing he could have pulled out of the bag, and I told him so. I knew he tended to assess everything through the prism of his ideal philosopher, but, as everyone knows, Wittgenstein had such self-destructive urges that, in everything associated with him, the ideal and the self-destructive are irreparably intertwined, which Mara had never denied though he always claimed to view things from the aspect of his Wittgenstein ideal. Mara didn't go anywhere but sat down at the table again and began vehemently defending not only his own *riverside stumblings* but also the heroic tale of how Wittgenstein struggled with reality and put his life on the line at the front (*no, I wasn't looking for trouble, and neither was Lud-de, he would never...* In the past, Mara had had difficulty accepting Wittgenstein's nickname, and even today, whenever he let it slip out like this, one could assume he was a little beside himself), indeed, the very fact that a philosopher could put his life on the line gradually began to affect his incomplete work, the work that was to become the *Tractatus*, shaping it in a singular direction that eventually made the whole work a singular achievement and all manner of other things. To Mara, this was a heroic tale of how thought can respond to turmoil and destruction, whereas I had always been opposed to such tales of philosophical heroism that could barely conceal the self-destructiveness at their root. On the face of it, it seemed as though the twenty-seven-year-old young man was *deliberately trying to get himself killed*, just as it now seemed as though Mara was looking for trouble, or something worse still, as I told him again. He was doing this, latching on to these fantasies because his mother's death, the funeral, the Ethiopian and his disappearance had really *unsettled* his life, and in fact he was behaving as though he too was trying to get himself killed... I hadn't finished my sentence before Mara interrupted me, *no, he wasn't looking for trouble, he was looking for the Ethiopian, and Wittgenstein wasn't looking for trouble either, rather circumstances began to shape the work he was*

undertaking... Whenever we talked about Wittgenstein, there was always a hint of jest, at least from
Mara. During our walks along the shore at Kaivopuisto, we'd argued about this many times, but now
we were talking about his *riverside stumblings*, which
had taken place only a few days earlier, and what
was true of Wittgenstein's self-destructiveness was
now also true of Mara's self-destructiveness... In the
spring of 1916, when Wittgenstein had already been
working on his forthcoming *Tractatus* for some time,
he arrived at the eastern front where he joined a unit
of the Austrian army positioned north of the River
Dniester in the borderlands between modern-day
Ukraine, Moldova, and Romania. Soon thereafter,
he asked his commander if he might be assigned to
the most dangerous of places, according to Mara this
was some sort of observation post where he would be
a sitting duck for enemy fire. Wittgenstein's wish was
duly granted, and he was sent to the observation post
for the night. Enemy fire was heaviest at night, and
the observation post was the most dangerous place
he could have been given. After surviving his first
night, he spent the whole day waiting for the next
night, when he would once again be a target for enemy fire. High up in the observation post, he imagined
he was like *a prince in an enchanted castle*. He had
turned twenty-seven only a few days earlier. Most
nights, he thought he was going to die and prayed

to God for the fortitude to look death in the eye all night, while he was alone and the target of enemy fire. And it was over the course of those days and nights, Mara believed, that the *Tractatus* started to change, though its exact wording only burst onto the page a month or two later. As though it had a life of its own, Wittgenstein's work had expanded from the foundations of logic to the very essence of the world... As if the foundation of logic itself had been the target of nocturnal enemy fire and was transfigured by something that helped it survive. There were things in the world that simply made themselves manifest, they could not be put into words. Life is the world, and the meaning of life is the meaning of the world. To pray is to think about the meaning of life, that is, the world, and we cannot bend the events of the world to our will... Mara always said that the *Tractatus* was the best war book he'd ever read. He might even have been a little proud of the fact that he had understood this aspect of the *Tractatus* before others started writing about it more generally... A war book, why not indeed, and a good one at that, I always replied, or was it fundamentally a horror story about how man struggles against a superior adversary, his own self-destructiveness, if on this occasion with a happy ending, surviving.

But Wittgenstein had an extraordinarily *constructive* side too, one that came about at sunrise as he clambered down from the observation post, said Mara and straightened his back on the other side of the table. This was the second time that Wittgenstein had prayed to God for fortitude. This time, he needed the courage to look his comrades in the eye, men who were not only drunks but profoundly stupid and violent. These utterly malicious and heartless men, lacking in the slightest trace of humanity, hated him because he had come to the front voluntarily and, moreover, voluntarily asked to be sent to the worst of all places… Mara gesticulated as though he were wiping breadcrumbs from the table.

Well, there you have it, I said, when the war hero or whatever he is comes down from the observation post the following morning, he doesn't understand that he sees his own self-destructive urges projected in other people, the same urges that took him up into the observation post in the first place… But Mara's heroic, philosophical tale continued. Three years later, after over a year as a prisoner of war, Wittgenstein returns to Vienna, still wearing his tattered old military uniform, and continues to use it for several years to come. His father had very wisely protected the family's assets by investing in American stocks and shares, and as a result of changes in the global economy, when war broke out Wittgenstein was one of the wealthiest private citizens in Europe, possibly even after the war too, there are conflicting claims about this, but in any case he was immeasurably affluent. Soon, a few weeks after returning to Vienna, he decides to give away his entire fortune. He would give up everything he owned, irreversibly, and in such a way that there would be no possibility for him to change his mind in case he came to regret his decision later on. This shocked his family and, indeed, everyone who heard about his plans. His family lawyer described it as financial suicide. Von Wright thought Wittgenstein a borderline case, and I assume this episode must have been a major reason why, Mara always said. People reacted to Wittgenstein's decision as though he was half-mad, if not fully mad, but that isn't the whole truth. By giving away all his inherited wealth, he maintained ties with his family, yet simultaneously managed to remove himself from it, which might sound insignificant though it is anything but. This was Mara's favorite argument. It's just that we don't think of deeds like this as a price worth paying for anything, he said. On the contrary, we think that hoarding wealth is a prerequisite for an independent life and, indeed, for the very continuation of life. For us, the obsession with hoarding wealth is the price of making sure that the individual remains sovereign and independent. Of course, when Wittgenstein relinquished all his wealth, he wasn't yet Wittgenstein, the philosopher. He had only written a short treatise that nobody wanted to publish. In retrospect, this episode is easily misunderstood; people see it as a heroic deed, which is entirely false, because that would mean the deed didn't have a tangible price, said Mara. When Wittgenstein gave up his inheritance, he was liberated from the grip of his family, but he had decided to abandon philosophy too, he wanted to get a home of his own and set about acquiring a practical profession, said Mara. While I was stressing about what might happen to the Kontula apartment, whether I'd end up out of pocket and what have you, I realized once again that Wittgenstein did things on *a completely different scale* than I would ever be able to do, just as he did when he gave up his enormous fortune, which turned out to be very good for his thinking, if not wholly indispensable, *whereas I'm just trying to find the Ethiopian,* he said and stood up from the table to *finally answer the call of nature.*

Thinking is the act of looking ahead. At the age of sixteen, Mara spent an entire summer sitting at his desk in Kontula reading philosophy from the early hours of the morning. His family lived in the adjacent housing complex, but the yard, the lawns, the swings and even a small patch of woodland were shared with our house, so my seven-year-old brother was out in that yard too, learning to ride his bike. He would ride up and down the same stretch of dirt track, behind the lawn about thirty meters from Mara's window.

Every day I walked across the yard to Mara's place, sat beside him at his desk and watched my brother cycling back and forth in front of the window. Every day he managed to go a meter or two further, and when he wobbled and fell, he walked the bike back to the start of the dirt track and tried again. Back home, my brother was encouraged in his cycling with almost exactly the same words he had said to me in Uunisaari earlier this spring, *look ahead* and *just look around a bit*... Sixteen-year-old Mara talked about philosophy in much the same way. He was the first in his family to wake up, and he began his mornings in the same way that he claimed G.E. Moore had started his, he held his right hand in the air, and doubtless his other hand too. *This is my hand, and this is my other hand.* Mara explained that Moore believed there were some things we could know with certainty, though in fact Wittgenstein had already *slain* Moore's claims, and to Mara, Moore's gesture meant something else altogether, for instance the idea that if any trifling matter can *unsettle* one's life, then we need to build something certain and reliable, something that nothing will be able to unsettle. A few years later, I saw facsimiles of Ludde's illegible handwriting at the university library almost daily; it looked like the needle of a seismograph following thoughts that appeared with difficulty, distorted, deformed, barely recognizable, as Wittgenstein was always complaining, and all the rises and falls of that handwriting revealed that the man behind them was *constantly on the verge of despair*, as I once said to Mara. Years later I felt as though that handwriting, turning and twisting like rapids in a mountain stream, only found its proper, almost happy context in Skjolden, surrounded by rocks, birch logs, pines, clear streams and the dark waters of the fjord. I was in Bergen, and because I had some spare time, I decided to undertake an overnight excursion to Skjolden in Sognefjord, primarily for the landscapes, the only place where Wittgenstein had ever found the ideal conditions for his work, as he put it. Skjolden was the only place where there was nothing to *unsettle* his life; everywhere else he always felt as though he was in the wrong place. Even many years later, Wittgenstein said that in Skjolden he brought new movements in thinking to life, paths of thought that were entirely his own. Thinking is the act of looking ahead, I remembered on the evening I arrived, as I stood on the hillside, still slippery from the rain and which began almost in the very center of the village of Skjolden. Thinking is the act of watching your step, Mara used to say. Wittgenstein kept the cabin until his death, and even four months before he died, when he knew death was drawing near, he bought a ticket to Bergen in order to settle in Skjolden, at the heart of winter, in the dark and cold. It was as though he went to Skjolden to die. I was staying in the center of Skjolden, in a rather drab and noisy hotel. The morning after my arrival, I woke early and was the first to arrive for breakfast where a woman, whom I'd met at the reception desk the previous evening, was busy organizing the buffet table, there was salmon everywhere, a dozen different kinds, all prepared in myriad different ways. I nodded at the buffet and said something about the array of salmon, the woman chuckled *ingenting er så godt for hjernen som en skikkelig feit laks.* She recommended a few rivers for salmon fishing and the salmon museum, which was excellent, apparently. That evening I'd seen a group of men in fishing garb in the hotel lobby, lures dangling from the brims of their hats, *så godt for hjernen*, I thought now. The woman was in a good mood, clearly an early riser, and reiterated that fish oils were excellent, especially salmon oils, then gave her forehead a knowing tap, *fantastisk sunt.* Right after breakfast, I set off to find the foundations of the cabin that Ludde had felt was suitably *in der Einsamkeit.* The location was high on a cliff above a lake right at the end of the fjord. The woman from the reception probably had no idea why I was in Skjolden, but she'd mentioned that the river that flowed into the lake just in front of

9 Norwegian: "there's nothing as good for the brain as a nice, oily salmon."

10 Norwegian: "terribly healthy."

my destination had once been one of the best salmon rivers in the area until in the 1950s and '60s a power station was built by the riverbank further upstream, and nowadays they couldn't establish a salmon population, even artificially, *it's all been ruined*, she said with a shake of the head. In Wittgenstein's day, there was no bridge across the river, so people had to row across the lake instead. After the bridge, a small footpath led off through the thicket, next to it a wooden signpost with the word *wittgenstein* carved into it with a knife. The footpath led to the wooded cliff top where the cabin had once stood. All that was left of it were its stone foundations, a few birches standing next to it, a few grey planks on the ground, shards of glass, down in the fjord the water was green and clear, ethereal, the summits of the mountains rose two kilometers into the sky. *One of the most beautiful places I've ever seen*, as I told Mara, though the cabin was demolished in the 1950s, and in its place there was now a pole bearing the Austrian flag, which was utterly shocking. The salmon had disappeared from the nearby river, only to be replaced with a salmon museum where one day Ludde would have a corner all of his own, Mara and I concluded.

A few years later I was passing through Vienna, and when, on the day I was supposed to leave, I went to Kundmanngasse to see the building that Wittgenstein had sketched, the shock was even greater than the one I'd experienced in Skjolden. The building was completely dead. I simply could not fathom what had been going through the architect's mind, even taking out an entire ceiling simply to increase the height of a room by three centimeters. For nothing. The house was the polar opposite of all life. Just to be sure, Ludde had refused anything that might have made the building agreeable, carpets, curtains, chandeliers and the like. Even from out in the street, one could see that nobody could ever enjoy themselves in the building, not even the flies, the ants, or the horses of the Red Army when, once Vienna was occupied after the war, the house was used as a stable. The building was a monument to the philosopher's ancestry, a giant urn. The oldest of Wittgenstein's four brothers disappeared on a boat trip in the Chesapeake Bay in circumstances that led the family to consider his death a suicide. This was then followed by another brother's suicide in Berlin, the third shot himself during the dying days of the First World War, and the fourth, who had dedicated his life to becoming a concert pianist, lost his right arm in the war, which was such a great loss that there was simply no point committing suicide. Nonetheless, the thought of suicide plagued both Ludwig and his one-armed brother so regularly that it was pure luck that neither of them ended up taking their own life. A wholly incapacitated family, as I told Mara, and the house on

Kundmanngasse was a monument to that incapaci-tation. It doesn't remind us of Wittgenstein's think-ing but of his childhood and family, not of what was so *constructive* about him, but of what he spent his entire life trying to put behind him and eventually prompted him to flee to the fjords of Norway. After visiting Kundmanngasse, I understood the things I'd heard about Ludde in a new light. Children are an impediment to thought, Wittgenstein told Jori Henrik, and encouraged him to leave his children in Finland when he joined him in Cambridge, perhaps this wasn't entirely to do with Wittgenstein's homo-sexuality but something else that I'd encountered at Kundmanngasse. Once my train had left Vienna, I sat in the dimly lit carriage, looked at the darkened landscape beyond the windows and concluded that, ultimately, humans have an infinite capacity for de-struction but far fewer resources for reconstruction, and now, at that table in the corner of the pub, I was worried Mara was looking for something that would unsettle his life, as I told him when he returned from the bathroom shaking the water from his hands.

Pff, I'd just decided I wanted to find the Ethiopian … And then, this was only on Monday, around this time in the evening… Mara told me he was in a car with a scholar of medieval history in the south of the city, heading to Villa Lante for some event or other, when

he noticed they were about to pass a place where the
Ethiopian might be found. Annika, I remembered the
scholar with a little help from Mara... He asked her
to pull over by the grassy verge at the side of the road.
This was a well-known cruising area, there's an abandoned old grain silo, Via Appia Antica runs past it, an
altogether unpleasant place. Annika agreed to wait in
the car for a moment, and Mara headed off toward
Appia... As he was speaking, I imagined the heat, the
smoke, the fragrance of the trees, the distant shouts,
laughter. He walked a hundred meters or so, veered
off the pathway and climbed up the embankment
into a straggly woodland (you had to watch out for
trash and all kinds of shit, he said) until he arrived
in front of a brick archway standing several meters
tall. A sleeping bag and a few dirty blankets lay on
the ground, inside the archway the soil was hard and
sandy, by the wall there was a camping stove and a
plastic bottle of ethanol or kerosene... I stood there
in the dusk, said Mara, I could smell the cool air, the
damp, the moss, and my mind was filled with childhood memories of the family summerhouse in Inkoo. I closed my eyes, and for a moment I imagined
I was in the potato cellar underneath the house, it
was extraordinarily moving, everything flooded into
my mind with such captivating power, I don't know
how long I'd been standing there when all of a sudden something altogether unreal happened, I heard

a voice calling my name, and the voice said *Martin*, just like when I was a child in Inkoo, not Mara but *Martin*. It was Annika, she was fed up waiting and had come looking for me. Together we walked back to the car, but after that I couldn't get my thoughts away from Inkoo, where I always spent time with my family, and before my uncle left Finland he too used to visit us there every summer. I'd been thinking about him a lot recently, without him I'd never have started doing philosophy, or anything else for that matter. My uncle wasn't much of a thinker, but he never held thinking in disdain either, and of all my relatives he was the only one who encouraged me and said that I'd chosen a good discipline and that people ought to spend a lot more time thinking, said Mara. My uncle always behaved as though he knew more about the ways of the world than other people, though even as a child I realized that he didn't actually know all that much, though he'd seen a lot. After all, he'd left Finland when he was young, he'd been to Costa Rica and spent many years in the Gulf of Mexico. In all these years, he's only visited Finland four times, said Mara. I thought about him many times as I stood there washing all my laundry and realized that *if it hadn't been for my uncle I would never have stumbled upon the Ethiopian.* The thought was already on my mind that night while the Ethiopian was sleeping next to me, snoring out his stupor. In my

unpacked suitcase he'd noticed a bottle of Koskenkorva vodka that I'd bought at the airport and asked if
he could crack it open, he said it was some anniversary or other, it was exactly a year or two since he'd arrived in Italy, then he blurted out that he's really from
Ethiopia though the night before he'd told me he was
from southern Italy. First he lied about being Italian,
and judging by his appearance he could easily have
been from somewhere in the Heel of Italy, then just
as we're about to go to sleep he tells me he's not from
Italy at all but from Ethiopia, and when I realized he'd
deliberately pulled the wool over my eyes I got quite
angry, said Mara, and when he noticed I was getting
angry, he took it all back, said he's half-Italian, said
his father or one of his grandparents or what have
you, one of them was Italian, but I didn't want to talk
about it, I was just too incensed. He passed out almost immediately, I couldn't get to sleep. I was livid,
and all the while I was trying to hold back tears, not
for myself, not because of his little lie, it was something altogether different. Of course, I understood
that at that moment an avalanche of emotions, pent-
up for days, was finally starting to move within me,
said Mara. I held back the tears, but emotions started
pouring out of me with a furious, utterly uncontrol-
lable power. The Ethiopian was asleep, oblivious, and
I lay awake, thinking about everything that had happened. If it hadn't been for my uncle, I wouldn't have

been there. If it hadn't been for my uncle, I wouldn't have had the inclination to read anything remotely noteworthy. There was a path leading from Kontula and from all those books, and that path had led me to where I was right then. My mother couldn't abide the fact that I read poetry, that I read *Björling*, said Mara. Why don't you do something useful with your time, she used to say, and later on she couldn't abide the Somali immigrants either, they didn't work, they did nothing that would stand the light of day, didn't live on a when-in-Rome basis, just like people used to say of Björling, he didn't work either, he did nothing that would stand the light of day, didn't live on a when-in-Rome basis, especially not in well-heeled Kaivopuisto where he was able to live for free in a small sauna, and on top of all this his poems were utterly unintelligible, so whenever Björling came up in conversation with anyone other than my mother I would explain that back in his day people in Finland used to think of Björling in much the same way as people think of the Somalis in Finland today, both equally unintelligible, only this time it wasn't a Somali lying next to me but an Ethiopian, Mara smiled and downed the remains of his Guinness as we stood up and walked out of the pub.

And only half an hour after the episode at the brick archway, I was at Villa Lante surrounded by people clinking their glasses, which felt incomprehensible, my thoughts were still caught up with the Ethiopian and the brick archway — it felt as though I was watching everything happening right next to me from a distance of a hundred meters, Mara continued. An obscure scholar from Helsinki University was giving a talk about some obscure subject or other, which gave a distinctly obscure impression of the whole university, but amid all the clinking I laughed for the first time in ages, I mean, really laughed... We turned onto the pedestrian bridge taking us across to Trastevere on the other side of the river. *By the way*, there's a party at Lante this evening too, said Mara, and pointed at the white building standing proudly atop the green hillside. I told him I didn't have the slightest intention of going, neither to Lante nor the party. Back when Mara was still doing philosophy, he didn't go to parties. He even complained about the amount of time he and his group of academics had wasted at the prime minister's residence. We were still on the bridge, people around us walking in both directions, beneath us a row of white tents stood along the riverbank, the sun setting up ahead gleamed above a large yellow-brown building, to my knowledge this was the Spanish embassy, and next to it was a church whose forecourt gave a panorama out over the city. Behind these buildings, the street led to Gianicolo, where Villa Lante was located. *Very well, that far, but not a step further*, I smiled and

pointed to the embassy building in front of us. Mara
sniggered in that Finland-Swedish way, meaning I
couldn't tell whether he was taking my objections
seriously or whether he was still planning to lure me
to Lante despite my reluctance. He recommended
we eat at a nearby restaurant run unaltered by the
same family for decades, or so he said. We arrived at
a small square with a couple of trees and too many
parked cars. In the corner of the square, a few tables
had been set out, next to them was an open door,
and standing in the doorway was a man in his sixties,
gaunt and with a sharp Roman nose, he barked instructions at his family members waiting the tables
and occasionally spoke to the diners, always in the
same gruff tone, as he examined the streak of sweat
running down the front of his shirt. He wasn't necessarily unfriendly; he simply didn't have the first idea
about manners. *Tables are all taken, come back in
half an hour... There'll be room in half an hour, people
come and go. Can I make a reservation?* Mara asked,
and the man nodded. Mara gave his name, and the
man turned toward the kitchen without saying a
word. The restaurant's interior wall bore old black-
and-white photographs of people eating platefuls of
pasta at the very same restaurant. I noted that the
restaurant's name was Il Mulino. I suggested we go
to the piazza in Trastevere. On the way, we heard
the odd word of Finnish, and Mara went quiet. He

didn't want our table to turn into some kind of drunken Little Helsinki, he said after we'd walked on a short distance.

Hundreds of people were thronging through the piazza. It seemed as though everyone who had been walking along the nearby streets with an open can of beer in their hand was now right here. Behind one group of people a wolfhound ran loose, it looked thin, malnourished, trotted along behind its master with a branch or stick clenched horizontally between its teeth, its thirsty tongue drooping to the side. The dog seemed like the only faithful creature in the whole square.

In front of Santa Maria in Trastevere stood a group of men in dirty sweatshirts who soon walked into the basilica through the left-hand door while another line of swarthy, unshaven men staggered out of the church carrying bags full of food. Mara and I stepped aside, the doors to the side aisles were open, and through the doors we saw the dusky interior of the church and the golden mosaics that caught the meager light filtering inside. It seemed as though some kind of service was going on inside, a handful of poor-looking people sat on the pews, but there was something curious about the singing, which was coming from a tape; the language sounded like Russian. I tried to listen carefully, to see whether the language might be Croatian, Czech, or Polish, but it was Russian, there was a wooden plinth on both sides of the altar, each bearing an icon and a few candles. How could these two denominations, whose paths had split centuries ago, exist under one and the same roof? A church volunteer was standing next to the doorway and I asked him about the Russian singing, but he smiled and said he didn't have any *information* on the matter.

Perhaps what I saw and heard in the church or the wolfhound running loose outside reminded me of Herling's book, which I'd been reading not only that morning but late into the previous night in Helsinki. One of Herling's longest friendships began in the sauna in the prison camp, and it all started with a piece of soap. Someone in the sauna stole Herling's scrap of soap, and he swore in Polish. A grey-haired man beside him asked in the same language, do you happen to know a poet by the name...? Herling replied that he did not know the poet personally but had read his works. In that case, you can scrub my back, the man beside him chuckled. The man then proceeds to tell his life story as Herling washes his back. The man and his young wife had both been sentenced to ten years, he explained. By the next day the three of them, Herling, the man and his wife, were the very best of friends. The young woman was from Łódź, the couple had a shared passion for

Polish literature, indeed it was this passion that had originally brought them together, led to their marriage, and in fact it was Polish literature that had got them convicted. For three years the couple heard nothing of each other, but now, recently, defying all probability, they had both ended up at the Kargopol camp, where this Romeo and Juliet of the gulag were unexpectedly reunited (which one of them saw the other first? Herling doesn't tell us this). What an unimaginable joy it was to lay eyes on each other again, to have shared moments together, spend entire evenings together. They even succeeded in being moved to the nearby Yertsevo camp at the same time. How did that happen? A stroke of luck? Unheard of in the annals of the gulag. Whenever possible, the woman followed her tired and helpless husband, he was weakened, exhausted, he'd soon be in the infirmary. She spent her days sorting sacks and vegetables in the kitchen storeroom, each day pilfering a potato or a piece of salted cod and sneaking it to her husband. On sunny mornings Herling and the man could be seen sitting for a moment on a bench next to the barbed-wire fence. They recite poems from memory, teach them to each other, this becomes their morning exercise routine... After three months, the man was sent to another camp. They received news that he was starving to death, wouldn't wash, and when he wasn't drowning in apathy he could be found begging outside the kitchen. One prisoner smuggled out a dirty scrap of paper, the man's final message to his wife. The message sent greetings to Herling too, the man explained that he had finally learnt to understand Hamsun.

We walked from the piazza back to the restaurant. The sharp-nosed man was still standing in the doorway. Mara glanced at his watch; exactly half an hour had passed. He asked the man if there was a table, but the man shook his head. When Mara reminded him of the reservation, the man simply shrugged his shoulders. Let's go over there, Mara turned to me and nodded toward another restaurant in the square, that one's much better anyway, he said. This restaurant was called Casetta something or other, and a moment later we sat down at a table for two. High above us ran a rope with laundry hung out to dry as a design element. I was about to point this out to Mara, *looks like it's laundry day here too*, but perhaps he wouldn't have found the sight of underpants fluttering with the air conditioning remotely amusing.

I realized I hadn't eaten anything since the bowl of salmon soup I'd grabbed before the flight. I'd left the house early at around 5 A.M. and taken a taxi through a deserted Helsinki and out to the airport. The taxi driver, a man in his sixties, talked incessantly about his travels in the United States. Nowadays, Eero Saarinen's Gateway Arch in St. Louis apparently looks more like the McDonald's logo with one arch missing, but he'd also seen the French Quarter in New Orleans before Hurricane Katrina and had liked that a lot. The levies wouldn't have given way during the hurricane if the National Guard, who had been looking after them until then, hadn't been halfway across the world occupying Iraqi oil fields, he said. His daughter was married to an Italian man and lived near Rome, he was planning a visit, he'd never been to Italy before. I told the taxi driver I was supposed to go to Italy in April, but then came 'Ash Thursday.' First I postponed the trip, then I cancelled it altogether once I realized that the five-day forecasts and even the 18-hour forecasts of the ash cloud were completely unreliable. On some days, three quarters of the 20,000–25,000 flights in European airspace were grounded. By mid-April, enormous clouds of ashen gauze were being carried by the winds from Iceland across the rest of Europe, reaching Scandinavia, the Balkans, and the British Isles. Then, the very next week, oil starts belching into the Gulf of Mexico, said Mara as I told him about the taxi driver. Depending on the wind and the currents, the oil that burst out of the seabed in the Gulf of Mexico either rose directly to the surface and formed enormous slicks, or it drifted a few hundred meters beneath the surface in giant layers the size of Manhattan. There wasn't supposed to be any risk of an accident, as we were told only shortly before the accident, yet about a dozen rig workers were killed, said Mara as we sat at the restaurant table. When I was younger, I dreamt of traveling to Louisiana because my uncle was there drilling for oil, said Mara. Life there was different back then, but now these two catastrophes, a hurricane and an oil spill, had turned the whole area into the gates of Hell. My uncle always used to say that oil rigs were the safest places on earth. It was much safer on a rig than on land. On land, people get greedy, he said. Life on the rigs is peaceful, though under the seabed there is an endless amount of oil and gas. The seabed is pocked with abandoned drill holes, at least 25,000 of them, and that's just the start, my uncle once said. In all those years, he sent only a few postcards, one from Mexico with a photo of an enormous cactus, its columns standing ten meters tall, like a cluster of organ pipes all tangled together. In front of the cactus stood a man and a horse. Compared to the cactus, the horse looked like a pony and the man like a dwarf, though both were of average size. The second time, he sent a postcard from Bourbon Street in New Orleans in which open balconies on three floors ran on both sides of the street as far as the eye could see. On the back of the card, he wrote that he'd spent the evening at a bar, and underneath this ran the words *She was so blonde*. The oil rigs were only a few dozen kilometers from the Louisiana coastline, where there were pelicans, swampland, and giant, rusting cranes amid the endless glades and rushes, as my uncle said. Now in that very same water, oil clung to the waterfowl's feathers, making the birds so heavy that they slowly sunk beneath the surface. The dolphins behaved as though they were drunk, they jumped up through the slick and sprayed black fountains of oil and water from their blowholes high into the air. At least my uncle didn't have to witness that, said Mara. His uncle visited Kontula that same summer when Mara was sitting by his window reading philosophy, and when at the end of the visit he accompanied his uncle to the bus stop, we met out in the yard, and my brother was there too, on his bike. They stopped to exchange a few words, and his uncle helped my brother to ride his bike, he held the saddle from behind and encouraged him, *once you get the hang of it, you'll never forget how to do it*, he said, as if he was talking about his life out in the Gulf of Mexico. My uncle was the black sheep of the family, said Mara, he cut ties with our relatives, or rather, he almost let our other relatives do it for him, and my relatives all had quite a tense relationship with him. I mentioned my own brother to Mara, I'd already told him about the situation back in the spring, but he wasn't listening. At least my uncle got to live in a world that's still just about on its feet, said Mara eventually, though his final years were terrible.

When Mara and I met up in Kaivopuisto four years ago, he told me he'd learnt the previous evening that his uncle had been beaten to death in his apartment in Las Palmas, where he had moved some time earlier. Somebody from the foreign office had informed him that the suspect had been apprehended and was in police custody, but Mara still didn't know who the perpetrator was or even whether it was a local or one of the many Finns living in Las Palmas. The first message said that his uncle was unlikely to regain consciousness, then came a second message saying that he had passed away, as Mara explained by the shore at Kaivopuisto. His uncle had been living in Las Palmas for just under a year. He was still awaiting a decision about his permanent-residence status and the benefits that this entailed. He had got to know a lot of the local Finns, who could often be seen in their own bars (the Finland Bar, the Anchor Bar, Pete's Pub), and because he spoke good Spanish, he was always asked to interpret whenever someone had a car accident or there was a disagreement over an apartment rental. By the next time I met Mara, his uncle had already been cremated and the urn transported to Finland, all courtesy of the Spanish state. The honorary consulate had mentioned that his uncle had been beaten to death with an iron bar, though not in his apartment, as initial reports had suggested, but at the city's long sandy beach, and from there his uncle had managed to drag himself back to the apartment. This catastrophe in the Gulf of Mexico has made me think of my uncle quite often, said Mara as we sat at the restaurant. When I saw dolphins, birds, and some unidentified furry animals, perhaps they were manatees, being put out of their misery with an iron bar along the Louisiana coastline, it reminded me of my uncle, he said there at the table. Back in Kaivopuisto, Mara said he didn't plan to attend his uncle's funeral, said he couldn't face his relatives, *but a curious thing happened, and I ended up saying goodbye to my uncle somewhere altogether different*, he said now, I'd decided not to attend my uncle's funeral, then at around the same time I read in the paper that my old university professor had died. I called an old friend and asked him to add my name to the book of condolences, but he said I'd have to come to the funeral. *Everyone would be there, and I would be more than welcome.* Instead of going to my uncle's funeral, I went to my former professor's funeral. Instead of being surrounded by people who had made my life difficult, I was with people with whom I'd spent some of the best moments of my life. I sat right at the back of the church and looked at the tufts of white hair on the second and third rows from the front on the left side of the aisle. This really was the international walking-stick brigade, united in silence, serious, *together*, though in fact they all disagreed about everything, and if this had been any other occasion, they would have been in a vocal argument with one another, but at least for those few moments the deceased was briefly forgiven for all the logical and human mistakes for which those gathered had once found him responsible. Mercifully, the floral tribute was silent, which spared us the lengthy eulogies in multiple languages. At the wake, I was sitting at the same table as an internationally acclaimed logician, who even at the age of ninety was still doing the rounds on the lecture circuit and seemed what one might call a little cheerily demented. *It should have been my turn,* he said, presumably meaning he ought to swap places with the deceased. At the front of the room, a couple of guests started reading out cards of condolences that had arrived from all over the world. It seemed at least every third signature was illegible as the two readers handed the cards back and forth, which is generally no help whatsoever. The logician took his white napkin, wrote something on it with a ballpoint pen, and handed it to the guest sitting next to him. *This is exactly how my name is written*, he said before calmly continuing to eat his sandwich cake. Another member of the walking-stick brigade leant over toward the logician: *I've started buying the* Guardian *to see whether another friend or foe has died.* The logician asked pointedly: *And which is it now?* The other man raised his eyebrows. *He was a*

very dear friend. Both in the church and at the wake,
I thought of my uncle. If it hadn't been for my uncle,
I wouldn't be sitting at this wake with some of the
world's most distinguished philosophers, listening
to them so intently that I accidentally dropped the
slice of cream pastry from my fork, making it land
upside down on the table, which was embarrassing,
until I saw the logician do exactly the same thing. In
their own ways, these philosophers helped me deal
with my uncle's death simply by talking about how
the world was already irrevocably doomed to ridicu-
lousness and, naturally, far worse besides. Just as my
uncle no longer had a place in the world, so thought
no longer had a place either. My uncle had tried his
best and done things that my other relatives hadn't
done, just as these philosophers had done their best
in their respective fields. But my uncle couldn't affect the course of things. He too deserved a funeral
with countless guests and wreaths. Like Wittgenstein,
my uncle too might have declared shortly before his
death that he'd had a wonderful life, said Mara as we
sat there in the restaurant. Many people think Wittgenstein must have been bitter to say that, maybe,
even my uncle had plenty of reasons for bitterness,
but at least he was able to live his own life, normally
people don't even try. Normally, people live someone
else's life, and first of all they are enslaved by their
parents. All things considered, emotions are quite

a burden, but without them we could give up on life without missing out on much. And so, my uncle had indeed lived a wonderful life. It was my uncle who made me realize I wouldn't swap my difficult emotions, or my difficult life for that matter, even if such a thing were possible. Even if we haven't had much love in our life, it's more important to have loved people and things, and I wouldn't swap that for the world.

I told Mara that if I hadn't been regularly visiting Turku from a young age, I would never have thought anything at all, and probably wouldn't even have started studying philosophy in the first place and would certainly not have progressed as far as, against all the odds, I did. Only Turku provided me with the ideal conditions for thinking, if indeed ideal conditions for thinking even exist, after all, Ludde wrote his *Tractatus* at the front, I said, and in Turku it was obvious from the start that books weren't considered some sort of secondary life, as people always say in Finland. Whenever I walked along the river, or anywhere else in the city for that matter, I sensed right away that books were the real life, compared to the steady din of drunken hollering that you could hear all evening in downtown Turku when I arrived in the city on Fridays, the same hollering continued through Saturday and into Sunday, as I left and headed back to Helsinki. I wouldn't have embarked upon anything unless at the age of fourteen or fifteen I'd started visiting my aunt in Turku, who even back then lived alone and at whose house I had a permanent room of my own where I could immerse myself in my own thoughts and what I was reading. Without Turku, I wouldn't have embarked upon philosophy, I said, if for no other reason than that my aunt offered me a safe place where I could immerse myself in my own thoughts. Thoughts never raced through my mind with such fervor as when I was a teenager in Turku, I said. Every so often, I had to close my book and go for a walk along the River Aura, which calmed me down and managed to slow my rush of thoughts. It was at that time, in fact, that I got the idea that when Wittgenstein was thinking, every now and then he had to submerge his head in a bucket of icy water. *My mind was on fire*, Ludde said of his time in Norway, and when I read his later philosophical fragments, they were like molten New Year's tin that had been tipped from a ladle and into a bucket of cold water. As early as my Turku days, I realized I'd been mistaken, Wittgenstein hadn't shoved his head into a bucket of water, it was Beethoven who would sometimes press his overheated head into a tub while he was composing, but the image of

11

11 A Finnish New Year's Eve tradition of heating a small amount of tin in a ladle, then pouring the molten metal into a bucket of cold water. When it hardens, the resulting tangle of tin is said to predict what will happen to the bearer in the year to come.

Wittgenstein and the bucket of water was persistent, and I still haven't managed to dispel it, I told Mara, just as I haven't been able to dispel the notion that von Wright, who was an unparalleled interpreter of Wittgenstein's works, was in fact interpreting New Year's tin, the tangled shadows it cast on the wall. *Now the shadow is a rabbit, now it's a duck.* Even the Ethiopian could say *my mind is on fire*, as I soon said to Mara, he too is living in the midst of a catastrophe, he doesn't have a place in the world either, he hasn't been able to keep up with the ways of the world, but, as it were, he's had to live at the whim of hopes and New Year's tin, for him the future is sometimes a duck, sometimes a rabbit, and in listening to Mara's laundry anecdotes I'd gathered that this was the case for all these people, the Wittgensteins, the Björlings, the uncles and Ethiopians, people who on the surface had nothing in common whatsoever.

Mara didn't sort people, just as the Wittgensteins, Björlings, and uncles of the world didn't sort people either. Mara couldn't stand the way we think of illegals as poor, pathetic souls just because they're in need of help. Mara didn't even sort people inadvertently, such that people like so-and-so belong over here while people like such-and-such belong over there, to the extent that I knew from our walks along the shore at Kaivopuisto that, no matter what we

were talking about, Mara would always compare everything to the Björlings and the Wittgensteins, and
in fact most of what I remember he told me about the
Ethiopian, I remember specifically because of these
two men. Björling spent years, decades, living in a
hopeless dead end, which is what Mara now said
about the Ethiopian. When we were walking along
the shore at Kaivopuisto, Mara would always talk
about Björling whenever we approached the house
plastered in grey and brown where Björling had lived
in a small space originally intended as a sauna and
where the door opened directly outside, and though
right now Mara didn't have much to say about
Björling, my thoughts remained with the poet as
Mara continued telling me about the Ethiopian. I listened to Mara's story and thought about the Ethiopian, and in fact in the course of Mara's story Björling
and the Ethiopian always appeared in my mind in
tandem. *The only real measure of thoughts is their
courage*, said Mara, because the aim of all thought is
to help the fly out of the fly bottle, as Wittgenstein
wrote, that is, to alter a set of impossible circumstances. The objective of thought is to help someone
out of their provincial condition, regardless of whether that meant changing country or changing one's
own spiritual circumstances, Mara often said, and
because one usually pours a drop of beer into the
bottom of a fly bottle to lure the flies in, then the

comparison with the provincial condition rings true, right down to the beer. When a fly flies into a fly bottle, it tries to find its way out, to liberate itself from its glass-walled prison, and precisely because it's in such a panic to set itself free, it flies into the glass walls over and over again, unable to turn around and change direction. Ludde thought that a person shut away in a cell would behave in much the same way. If there is a row of fake doors in front of him, he will grab onto the same doorknobs over and over again, unable to turn around, even if the real door is behind him. Björling didn't rest his hand on the fake doorknob, said Mara, and I'd recognized when I was younger that Björling was plagued by the prevailing provincial condition perhaps more than anyone else in Finland. From one decade to the next, people said they couldn't understand his poetry, which naturally implied that there was nothing in his poetry to understand in the first place, though almost all his poems, particularly those deemed so unfathomable, are poems that help the fly out of the bottle and back into a normal, natural life. Björling teaches us everything about normal, natural thought, said Mara, though it was this very quality that meant that over the years and decades he'd ended up with a bloody nose time and again. Björling's poetry was derided as impossible to understand, though in fact its very *obegriplighet*, its unintelligibility, is a synonym for normal and natural life, because it is this same normal and natural life that is for most, if not all people, the hardest and most unintelligible thing of all, said Mara. For years and decades Björling's poems were considered unintelligible by the very people whose judgment was respected the most in Finland, said Mara. The very people, whose common sense was held in high regard, wrote that Björling was *deranged*, and there's no doubt that these same people's supposed common sense garnered a great many *plaudits* too. It's probably because of Björling that I feel such sympathy for the Ethiopian, though he put me in a terrible bind just when I had plenty of other things to worry about, Mara continued. What applies to Björling applies to the Ethiopian too, people are suspicious of him too, they reject him, don't want to understand him. He too is *obegriplig* and his life and existence are completely *obegripliga*. In fact, his life and existence are living synonyms for the word *obegriplig*, and whenever people say they cannot understand something, what they actually mean is they don't want to or don't have the slightest intention of understanding it, said Mara, just as Björling's poems weren't actually *obegripliga* at all, but people had decided that they didn't want or didn't care to understand him, even if he'd written the simplest things imaginable, as quite frankly he normally did. I was half-listening to Mara

12

12   Swedish: "unintelligible."

whose rant was escalating into full-scale fulmination, as it were, and I thought to myself that there was in fact one occasion in Björling's life when his poems became quite literally unintelligible, as Mara had a habit of pointing out. He mentioned the event almost every time we walked along the shore at Kaivopuisto and passed the place where Björling had lived after the war until his death and where he had lived before the war from around 1910 until February 1944, though in a different building from the one after the war, as in February 1944 something happened that Mara always called *the greatest catastrophe in Finnish literature* and sometimes *the most unparalleled catastrophe in Swedish literature* or even *the great catastrophe of European literature*. He was referring to February 1944, when the Russians had already ferociously bombed Helsinki on two separate occasions, and once dusk had descended on the evening of February 26, then began the third night of bombing, the most furious of all. At around eight o'clock that evening, the sky above Helsinki was full of Christmas-tree candles, as people called the glaring clusters of bombs that lit the evening sky and made it bright as day. Björling was in town and spent the night in an air-raid shelter underneath the Union Bank. At around seven o'clock the following morning, he hurried back to his home on Itäinen Puistotie. Both buildings on the plot had been destroyed.

At around two o'clock in the morning, at least one explosive had fallen on his house, followed at four o'clock by several firebombs, and by six o'clock everything had burnt to the ground. Everything that Björling had written over the last thirty years had been reduced to ashes, the thousands of papers, plans, sketches, materials, concepts, as he wrote in a letter to his brother in Sweden. The following Monday, two days after the devastation, the corner of the guttering, or what is left of it, is still burning when Björling returns to search the ruins for bundles of papers among the ashes. The floors of the building have all collapsed in on one another. Iron, junk, masonry, *is this what death is*, he writes in another letter to Lagercrantz. He returns to the house on several occasions. One day, he wades through a pile of rubble a meter deep, simply in order to stand between the walls above which his room once was. Now there is blue sky above him. He pulls out bundles of manuscripts and old newspapers, still smoldering, and covers them with bricks so as not to start another fire. The stairwell, which once led up to his apartment, is still there, except now the stairs don't lead anywhere. Björling only dares put his foot on the first step, in front of him is a heap of junk and rubble, everything around him is smoldering, smoking, and flaring up. Slightly further ahead, at the spot where the stairs turned forty-five degrees to the right, is the metallic banister that he could have gripped with his hand, had the stairs still been in place. Pieces of brick wall lie all around, twisted water pipes, in the yard is an upside-down bathtub, amid the debris the detached doorbell, he notices. At the neighboring house, all that is left are the walls decorated with pilasters. Björling searches among the roof tiles, the iron, the bricks and charred furniture for his papers, though they would disintegrate into ash in his fingers. On one scrap of paper he makes out the words "Sorglös går — nästa dag — döende." He manages to find a bunch of blackened papers which the heat has shrunk to half their original size, their surface is shiny, hard, and dark, but he can just make out the text on their surface. He keeps his small, charred papers in a shoe-box with silk paper between each of the pages. Over the following days, in his temporary accommodation on Hietalahdenkatu, using a magnifying glass, he tries to interpret the papers in the shoebox, which he has started to call his *ashen archive*. He tries to salvage whatever he can by deciphering individual words and guessing at the rest from the *voice of the ash*, as he calls it. On this one occasion, Björling's poems were genuinely *obegripliga*, in fact they were so *obegripliga* that he needed a magnifying glass to read them, and even then he was only able to read them during the daytime because you can't read ash-

13 Swedish: "walk carefree — the following day — dying."

es by candlelight, as he once pointed out. Björling returns to the ruins of the collapsed building several times, small fires flare up over the course of the coming weeks, and eventually there are no more papers to be saved. The greatest loss is without question the material that Björling had been planning to turn into a work of prose, the material was already written, all that remained to do was put it together at some point in the future, *sammanställa, icke skriva.* Everything [14] in the book was supposed to be spontaneous, experienced in the moment, so he couldn't rewrite those pages, he would never be twenty, thirty, forty, or even fifty years old again. There amid all the devastation, at the age of fifty-six, *upon this laundry day of his own, a day of ash and displacement,* for the first time in his life Björling is worried that now his poems really are unintelligible, that they were always so, as if the destruction of his entire life's work has revealed his writing to be futile, a failure. On the morning of February 27 Björling owns nothing but the dirty, ash-stained clothes that he happened to be wearing. He writes a list of things he needs, which he asks his brother to send from Sweden. Shirt (size 41 or 42), preferably unicolor, dark, 2 pairs of underpants, 2 sheets, 2 hand towels, 2 pillowcases, some handkerchiefs, a pair of shoes for the summer (to help save the winter shoes), 2 pairs of socks, some pairs of

14   Swedish: "compile, not write."

gloves (spring), a toothbrush, soap if possible, a hat for springtime, not too light (size 56). Two, pairs, and so on, as though he were making a list of small garments from Noah's ark. He still had to collect his own books; there weren't many copies of those in the world, for they were not deemed good enough. When the house is rebuilt, or rather two new buildings constructed to replace the two destroyed, Björling will be able to return to the same spot where he lived before the catastrophe. He will restart his life, hanging by nothing at all. He will again sit by the window and write. *Life, a squirrel leap.* There is a maple in front of the window, nowadays its trunk has split into three thick branches and its bough stands taller than the four-story house. It's unfathomable that the maple survived the bombing that night, though all around it everything else was razed to the ground, I thought as Mara and I walked past the spot last summer and stopped to watch a bungee crane by the shore standing 110 m tall where, every few minutes, someone jumped squealing from the top then bounced up and down on the cord, momentarily suspended above a platform floating in the sea, but now that Mara was talking about Björling and the Ethiopian almost in the same breath, the Ethiopian's life began to sound like pages destroyed in a bombing raid, pages it is impossible to read at all, let alone *sammanställa.* Björling's ashen archive formed a link to the Ethiopian's life; he too was hanging by nothing at all, *life, a squirrel leap* could equally apply to him, though we didn't actually know anything about this stranger's life, Mara didn't even know why the Ethiopian had left Ethiopia in the first place.

After the incident at the archway, I thought about these things a lot, and one evening I was reminded of a small sketch I'd seen in one of my childhood books, said Mara. There were grey trucks in the picture, each with a red cross on their side, in the middle of a barren, desolate landscape. The vehicles were Swedish. The landscape was Ethiopia, and the book, which was a children's book about world history, explained that in 1935 and 1936 the Italians had conducted airstrikes against a convoy of Red Cross vehicles in Ethiopia. I hadn't thought of that sketch, barely the size of a matchbox, for years, decades, yet now it suddenly appeared vividly in my mind, and I wondered how memories like this can lie dormant for decades then suddenly pop into your mind, said Mara, except naturally I'd been thinking about the Ethiopian and I'd recently read that vans from the Red Cross hand out food aid twice a week at a gravel pit behind Ostiense station where lots of homeless migrants live. This place wasn't far from my regular walk, and one day I decided to stop into Ostiense station. It was one of the first really hot days of the summer. Sweat was running down my back as I crossed the piazza in front of the station before eventually finding shade in the long colonnade running the length of the station building. I knew that construction of the station was completed around 1936, but I was still taken aback when I realized quite what kinds of mosaics I was walking on. They depicted various episodes from Roman history, and that history culminated in a dark figure, his right arm raised in a familiar salute. Behind the man, a flock of oil-black eagles were flying in formation, said Mara. Ever since I stopped doing philosophy, I'd wished for a life with responsibilities, but what I saw in that mosaic was a travesty of responsibilities, he said. Back in Kontula, I often began my mornings the way I imagined G.E. Moore had begun his mornings by raising a hand in front of me, but there at my feet one of the mosaics showed a black-caped imbecile raising his arm too. I'd done this in order to be able to perceive something about reality, this monstrosity was doing it because reality meant nothing to him, because he and his ilk are above such things and can even make the birds fly in formations of their choosing. When I was still doing philosophy, or trying to, I learnt to take a step or two forward, said Mara. You're supposed to point out things that other people don't care for, that they overlook, fail to see or fail to realize, and there I was, bemused that these mosaics had been there for decades as if nobody had even noticed them. I walked on from the station, and before long I saw the enormous gravel pit, which was like the giant crater left by a bomb, or perhaps ten or even a hundred bombs all at once, said Mara, there were tents and blankets draped across the concrete walls, and towering over the pit and the street was a row of nine-story apartment blocks built in the 1960s, and seen from the pit they must have looked like they were up in the sky. Their strip balconies were all full of assorted clutter, and looking from those balconies the pit probably seemed like it was at the bottom of a hellish abyss beneath them, which it was, of course. I'd read in the paper that the people who lived on the top floor of these apartment blocks were used to turning a blind eye to the homeless people down below, who nonetheless irritated and annoyed them, positively thrust themselves into sight, and the residents didn't at all like the fact that the Red Cross vehicles came to hand out food aid twice a week. From the street, a small path ran between tufts of grass to the shacks below, the kind of path that in Finland would lead to a construction site, the kind of path that would be lined with gravel so the trucks and diggers could pass easily. Down in the gravel pit, its perimeter demarcated by litter-strewn embankments and two concrete walls, was a row of dwellings cobbled together from dangling blankets, washing lines,

planks and scraps of plastic, in front of them a dozen
or so blue dome tents, about thirty people loitering
in little clusters, all between twenty and forty years
of age, and not a single woman in sight. Some were
sitting on white plastic deckchairs or upturned plastic baskets, further to the side there was even a white
couch and an armchair with a tall back, which might
have been better suited to one of the living rooms
in the apartment blocks rising high above the pit. In
front of them were a few fires, a large black pot had
been placed on a grate balanced upon some rocks,
and beneath it was an open fire. There was litter everywhere, empty plastic water bottles and disposable
plates. To one side, a young man was lying on a metallic bedframe where a folded grey blanket served as
a mattress. He glanced at me quizzically. I noted that,
despite the conditions and the indecent heat, he was
relatively sharp, dark-blue shirt, neatly trimmed hair,
and it couldn't have been very long since the last time
he'd shaved either. I asked him whether there were
any Ethiopians here, but he smiled and shook his
head. Why was he dressed so sharply, I wondered, especially at a time of year when even a short walk can
feel like an endless, sweaty trek. These people had left
their unknown homelands and crossed arid hellfires
far worse and more exhausting than this, goodness
knows how great a mental and physical price they
had paid, not to mention the financial cost, I thought

as I noticed a banner draped on the clothesline, like an extension of the laundry, bearing the words *rifugiati afghani*, Afghan refugees. I had come to Rome voluntarily and I had everything I needed, but these people's motivation for coming here under such circumstances was beyond all imagination, said Mara. We always assume people do things for the same reasons we do them, he continued. We imagine everybody else's life is the same as our life, but our life and someone else's life aren't on the same track, they're on parallel tracks, and there's a wall of unintelligibility running between them, he said. I didn't find the Ethiopian. Mara explained that he asked three different people living there if they knew anything about the Ethiopian. The answer was always friendly but negative. *In the past, you used to know where to find different people. Ma, al giorno d'oggi, c'è tutto confuso, mischiato*, said the third man, using hand [15] gestures to fill in the gaps in his language skills (Mara mimed the unknown man's hand gestures there in front of me, without noticing he was doing it). Before I turned to come back, I glanced behind the blankets, said Mara, and on a narrow strip of concrete there were a few foam mattresses. I wondered where these people went to the toilet, there were only a few tufts of grass on the embankments, but the bushes

15   Italian: "But, these days, everything's chaotic, a mess."

were so stunted, barely knee-high, and I don't think I could have brought myself to drop my pants and crouch down among them. Perhaps they waited until dusk and did what they had to under cover of darkness while looking up at the lights in the windows of the apartment blocks around them, in case someone came to the window or perhaps two or three residents appeared cheerfully smoking and chatting on the balcony, said Mara. Then I remembered reading in that same newspaper article that some refugees lived in the sewers by the station. Behind one of the blankets was the entrance to the station's main sewer, so it wouldn't be much problem to squat down there and go about your business, they simply shat in amongst everybody else's shit, said Mara. Later on, I heard that the locals called this place *La Buca*, the hole.

I don't know whether I'd gone to find the Ethiopian because the sketch from my childhood was creeping back into my mind, or whether the memory had come back specifically because I couldn't find him, Mara continued after a moment. In any case, this all made me wonder. The following day, when I happened to have some time in the afternoon, I visited the Swedish Institute in Rome, I know some people there, and asked if I could look over some of their databases. In the library, I found a book written by a man who had taken part in a Red Cross expedition

to Ethiopia in 1935 and 1936. An inexplicable wave of
emotions consumed me as I turned the page and,
without any warning, saw a black-and-white photograph of the expedition's five specially prepared Volvo trucks with the red crosses on their flanks, exactly
the same as the ones in the sketch I remembered
from all those years ago, said Mara. Soon, my attention was drawn to another photograph showing a
man sitting halfway up a steep mountainside. He was
sitting with his back slightly hunched, leaning against
the ragged rockface, and from his high vantage point
gazing out across the landscape opening up in front
of him. One could imagine the silence around him,
the faint breeze. He looked like a hermit sitting in
front of his cave, deep in his own thoughts. At first
glance he looked a lot like the young Jori Henrik, said
Mara. The man was the book's author, as I learnt
from the text underneath the photograph, and this
moment of contemplation was in fact anything but
peaceful, as the man in the photograph, one Gunnar
Agge, appeared to have a bugle beside him, which
was mentioned at some point in the book. It turned
out he was keeping watch over the horizon, where
Italian planes flew every day. Far beneath him, protected by the trees, were some tents, one or two
trucks, a great throng of people, infirmary staff and
patients who would all go into hiding as soon as they
heard the sound of the bugle from the cliffside

warning them of approaching aircraft. Mara recommended that I read Agge's book if ever I stumble
upon it, as he put it, and even suggested he could
borrow the book from the institute for me right away
so I could take it with me to Naples, where I was
heading for a few days, and I could return it to him
before my flight back to Helsinki, though, of course,
this was completely impractical, as I told him. It's a
book that sheds light on our times too, said Mara. If
you want to understand what's happening right now,
you must read Agge's book, he said. When I was
reading that book, I kept thinking of the Ethiopian
and how destiny is born of a film of pain stretching
across generations and our attempts to liberate ourselves from everything with which we are ultimately
burdened. As I read the book, I was taken aback at
the way in which people think they are living a
unique life in a truly unique age and can't see that the
world repeats precisely the same brainless acts again
and again, read the book as soon as possible, he
laughed. Only a few weeks later, in early August
when I was supposed to be working on something
altogether different, I ensconced myself in the great
reading room of Stockholm's Kungliga Biblioteket
with Agge's book for two days. I soon found the photograph Mara had mentioned, the one of the author
sitting with his head inclined slightly forward on the
mountainside, which at first glance looked as though

it was covered in swallows' nests. An empty panorama opened out in front of him, somewhere nearby were the tents that the Italian pilots hadn't seen, because a green tent under the green canopy of trees gives better protection than the flag of the Red Cross, as Agge wrote. The author seems pleasant. He never says anything superfluous about himself but writes in very concrete terms. It's no surprise Mara liked the book. There is something similar about them, I thought, Agge and Mara. In a stylistic departure for books of this kind, Agge doesn't even introduce himself or his background, and it was only once I started searching for information about him that I discovered he was born on November 9, and as these events took place in 1935, I calculated that he would have celebrated his thirty-fifth birthday at sea a few days before docking at Djibouti. He writes about everyday events. In Addis Ababa the Swedes split into two units, both of which have their own destination in southern Ethiopia. The first to set off is the main unit led by a Dr. Hylander. The unit led by Agge leaves the following day and spends the first night at a hotel by the shore of a small volcanic and very sulfuric lake, and it is after this that the real struggle begins. The members of the expedition have all manner of reasons for being involved, but Agge himself remains a mystery. He never explains precisely what he is struggling for. He writes about the heat and the sub-zero temperatures high upon the plains at night, the terrifying hills that their vehicles cannot climb, and in passing he mentions the breathtaking views. The cars are hauled across the rivers one at a time using a combination of logs and pulleys. The unit crosses vast stretches of pasture and marshland and finally arrives at a bridge that looks as though it will withstand far less than their three-and-a-half-ton truck. The bridge's main structure is made of poles fashioned from gnarled logs. Laid horizontally upon the poles is a set of wooden trellises, lined with flat blocks of chalkstone. Down below, the water churns its way along the riverbed. Agge steps onto the bridge, and a few stones fall through the trellises and into the water. They decide to try all the same. The belongings are unloaded from a lighter truck, which they picked up in Addis Ababa, and the truck slowly drives onto the bridge. As the vehicle progresses across the bridge, the tires cause more stones to fall from the structure, but as if by a miracle it arrives safely at the other side, where it is loaded up again. The bridge would not survive another crossing, so the Volvo truck sets off to find a shallower section where it can safely cross the river. A few kilometers further downstream is a promising-looking ford, and the truck cautiously drives out into the red earth along the embankment until the ground gives way and the truck nearly slumps onto its side. As the truck is hauled out of the mud, something in the gearbox breaks. Agge returns to the bridge, where thirty or so local men have started to fill the bridge supports and the entire river channel with rocks. The following day, work is still ongoing, but the Volvo's gearbox has now been repaired and the vehicle is driven across the water empty. The men carry the load across the river and a few extra kilometers along the opposite shore where the terrain is a steep incline and so wooded that the Volvo has difficulty moving forward even without its cargo. Eventually, the vehicle is loaded up again, and moments like this and a drop of the local honey mead help raise everybody's spirits. The following nights they spend high up in the mountains. The antifreeze in the vehicles' motors freezes up, and at night the wind is so biting that not even their thick Swedish blankets can provide adequate protection. The members of the expedition spend a few hours looking for scraps of wood to build a fire, without finding as much as a twig. At three o'clock in the morning, they finally give up. The following morning, Agge stacks the crates into a wall to protect them from the wind, and after many attempts he finally manages to light a fire beneath the camping stove to boil water for coffee. He writes about the wild olive trees, the *zigba* pines, and *hagenia* trees. The tree line is at an altitude of 3,000m, but plants flourish long after that. Agge discovers many *Swedish flowers* too,

bellflowers, dandelions, and cross-leaved heath. At
3,500m above sea level, bushes of cinquefoil still
stand taller than a man, gleaming yellow in the setting sun. The three-week journey feels like it lasts a
lifetime. Sometimes, a full day's struggle takes them
only 20km further onward. The trucks become lodged
in the gravel every few hundred meters, and even in
easier terrain, for the most part, they have to remain
in first gear. High up in the mountains, the earth
glints in the morning frost, Agge gets a cold and his
legs ache, and the pain only abates once they descend
to the sweltering rifts surrounded by vertical cliff faces. Agge writes about the people with whom he walks
along the riverbanks and fishes, unaware of everything that would happen to them and their carefully
tended farms in the years to come. Agge describes
the landscape of the colossal crater-like valley, the
mimosa, aloe, and agave plants, the different-sized
pepos, the acacias and stunted, withered cypresses.
He writes about the infernal power of the sun, the
thirst, the dried-up springs and lack of clean water. In
one of the springs, the water is full of salts, soda,
camel and donkey urine. Some members of the expedition are so dehydrated that they drink it. Later that
evening they lie on the sandy embankment, vomiting,
unable to move despite the swarms of grey mites
crawling over their skin. Eventually, the unit arrives
at its destination. Agge climbs to the top of a tall

promontory, the expansive landscape opening out beneath him. To the south is a mountain range, tinged in blue. Somewhere over there, beyond the mountains, are the Italians. Agge has reached his observation post, just as Wittgenstein climbed up to his own observation post on the eastern front and Björling crouched over his ashen archive. Agge believes in deeds. *The selfless, practical love that manifests itself through concrete acts is a language that all people understand right away.*

Agge knows nothing of Hylander's main unit which, after a lengthy detour, finally reached its own destination a mere 150 km to the south fully three weeks earlier. Their 1,300 km trek is nothing short of a miracle. As soon as the expedition arrives at its camp, the Swedes wade out into the nearby river, despite warnings that this stretch of the river is infested with crocodiles. The camp is set up near the embankment, where clusters of leafy palm trees provide respite from the sun. The trucks are parked prominently on display. Between the tree trunks they hang the flags of Sweden, the Red Cross, and Abyssinia, though the local flag is soon taken down again to avoid any confusion. The best thing to do is to start work with a clean slate or *a clean flag*, as the Swedes say. Two days before Christmas Eve, at eight o'clock in the morning somewhere in the distance, comes the sound of explosions, soon two aircraft are flying directly toward the camp. Hylander and Svensson remain standing in the middle of the clearly demarcated area. Then they see that one of the planes is dropping what looks like a bomb or bombs, and before the first plane is upon them, they hear a dull metallic thump. The men run into the bushes as a volley of machine-gun fire strikes the sand between them. The planes circle above the camp for around fifteen minutes until it looks as though they are about to make their departure, before one of them lets loose a shower of bullets that hit the ground only ten to fifteen meters from where the men are lying in the bushes. The following morning, again at around eight o'clock, another plane circles above the camp, then disappears. Down in the camp, there is a sense that the Italians have finally come to respect the Red Cross. Every day, aircraft appear above the camp, while down on the ground people continue to work without a break. The number of patients increases, among them many with severe injuries. Medical supplies begin to dwindle, and three Swedes decide to drive 300km to Negele to fetch medicines and supplies. They drive without a break for three days straight, only stopping once they reach Negele where, despite the darkness, they quickly load up the truck and set off on the journey back to the camp. One of the Swedes, Lundström, drives the whole way, over

600 km in total, a truly heroic undertaking, the others say. Exhausted, they arrive back at the camp at three o'clock in the morning with a fresh delivery of medical supplies. Four hours later, at half past seven, the Italians again appear overhead. This time the planes start bombing the camp itself. After this, the planes fly lower still and start firing at the tents, which are all full of bedridden patients. The whole camp is destroyed, half of the patients die, the dead and maimed lie all around. Lundström is still in the front seat of his truck. As the planes approached, he was still deep in morning prayer. A piece of shrapnel sliced off part of his jaw and now he cannot speak. In the book, there is a photograph taken three weeks earlier, as the expedition was about to set off from Addis Ababa. In the photograph, Lundström is standing by the truck, squinting despite his visor, his smile is flat, his jaw sturdy, though in all other respects he has a somewhat scrawny frame. At one o'clock, the first truck successfully leaves the camp. Hylander, covered from head to toe in mud and blood, Lundström, and the worst of the wounded patients are transported back along the same rocky, pot-holed road that Lundström has been driving for three days. The convoy has to stop several times to find water. They assumed the Italians wouldn't return that same day, as the motors of the engines on the Caproni aircraft were so weak that they could only fly in the

morning before the temperature rose and weakened their capacity. Hylander can neither eat nor drink, six pieces of shrapnel have mutilated him; they try to give Lundström some sugar water, this only succeeds once they stick a tube up his nostril to make sure a few drops trickle down his gullet. Lundström knows he won't survive. He can't speak, but he writes down his thoughts in a notebook, tears out a page and hands it to the others. On New Year's Eve at six o'clock, Hylander sits up in the back of the truck, knocks on the window at the back of the cabin and says *min kamrat har slutat andas.*

One hundred and fifty kilometers away, the author is sitting on the mountainside familiar from the photograph, though more probably he is doing his actual job taking care of the patients in the tents. The Italians haven't found this camp, and in these brief moments of respite Agge teaches himself to identify different species of dove and pigeon (the laughing dove, the speckled pigeon, the European turtle dove, the Namaqua dove, and the emerald-spotted wood dove), and sometimes he even spots a stork too. For the moment, the planes haven't yet discovered Elod, the settlement around them that Agge refers to as a town (in fact, even today the place is

16 Swedish: "My comrade has stopped breathing."

no larger than a modest village), but the expedition is worried about being uncovered. Soon, all those able to stand up from their beds hurry into caves or nearby woodlands in the mornings without waiting for the warning of approaching planes. Even those patients who can only crawl drag themselves into the cover of the trees. Everyone's thoughts are centered on the planes, and eventually the whole camp is moved into the woods. As darkness falls, people continue to work in the tents by the light of the kerosene lamps. Sometimes they sit outside the tents, and high above them is a belt of stars that not even the planes can shoot down. Inside the tents, however, medication is running out, food is in short supply, every day someone shoots one of the antelope grazing near the camp. Mara must have liked Agge, hiding in the darkness of the woods. Agge comes across as a quiet man who only occasionally smiles or laughs. In one of the photographs, the members of the expedition are crouched over the ground examining the ants. One day, Agge, afraid of being seen, watches as seven three-engine planes approach along the mountain ridge. Sunlight glints on their wings and propellers, but Agge concludes that the morning sun must be shining right into the pilots' eyes. Another day, three giant Capronis appear from behind the ridge and fly right above him. He hides in the bushes. The threat is always the same, if even one of the

Italian pilots were to look down, *there he was.* The noose was tightening day by day. One morning, five Italian planes appear to be heading straight toward the camp and the settlement, they fly overhead and bomb a deserted town on the nearby plains. The aircraft circle above the town for a long while, showering it with machine-gun fire. After the attack, the ground is covered with dozens of baboons, some freshly born, grimly mutilated by the bullets. It was as though in Italy gasoline, oil, and bombs grew on trees like oranges, writes Agge. Alongside these new fruits, he could add the mustard gas that smells of horseradish. This is the oil-like liquid that surrounds the bomb craters in a veil of droplets. Sometimes it explodes in the air and rains down like perfectly normal precipitation, then remains on the grass or even in the water for days. When a foot, shin, hand or palate comes into contact with this liquid, the skin comes out in large blisters. It makes the eyes sting so much that you can't open them. The burning air is choking, makes you cough. The grass and the leaves of the trees turn yellow, then wither away. After the bombing raids, people scramble blinded through the bushes, swaddled in an invisible yet boiling net that will not let go of its prey.

Hylander has recovered from his wounds, but his unit does not return to its former camp and, instead, three members of the expedition pay it a quick visit and report a terrible stench that could be smelt miles away. Hyenas and other scavengers have dug up the bodies hurriedly buried in the sandy embankments. At the beginning of April, Hylander and his unit join Agge at Elod, and together they look for a new camp-site on the mountainside. Following orders from Geneva, Hylander has had another Red Cross flag made. It is 196 m² in size and can be seen many kilo-meters from the ground. Not one of the bed patients or walking wounded dares come within a kilometer of the camp, so three well-hidden infirmary tents are erected a suitable distance away. Later on, the flag disappears, perhaps stolen, the patients probably thought it best to get rid of it. A month earlier, they apprehended a spy, a local Somali whose task it was to mark the settlement for the pilots using a length of white fabric. The Ethiopians hang the spy on the hilltop where the pilots are sure to see him. Every fifth day, there is a market in Elod (milk, durra, cof-fee, goats), and Agge recounts that on March 7, the familiar sound of a plane's motor returns in the after-noon when the market is at its busiest. Hundreds of people run into the woods for cover, but the plane ar-rives quickly and circles overhead for fifteen minutes. They have found Elod. Perhaps this time they have a

Somali guide on board, Agge ponders. At the regular time the following morning, nine bombers approach the camp but fly right past. Now the members of the expedition only work in the tents at night. Before sunrise, they carry the patients into caves along the mountainside, which provide at least some form of shelter. On March 13 at eight thirty, exceptionally late for Agge to be drinking his morning coffee, someone shouts, *they're coming now*. Agge runs into the woodland just as a plane appears overhead. He is well hidden, but the plane flies low above him and drops two heavy bombs that explode nearby. A moment later, a boy of around eight or nine appears out of the bushes and runs toward Agge, the boy is trembling and explains that the pilot saw him. Once before, in December, a plane had taken the boy by surprise out in the open ground, and the pilot had followed him. The boy had just reached the edge of the woods and hidden behind a tree when the machine guns opened fire, their bullets hitting the tree trunk and tearing up the leaves around him. Now the planes return every day. They drop bombs, fire their machine guns. Sometimes Agge hides in the cover of the woods, other times he cowers behind a termite hill out in the fields. He watches the planes as they swoop low over the camp. He can clearly see the smirks on the pilots' faces. Days pass one after another, identical. Flocks of vultures have learnt to follow behind the planes, Agge notes. One day, two planes painted with Ethiopian insignias appear in the sky above Elod. The bombs and machine guns are familiar, Italian. The planes drop splinter bombs on the Red Cross tents. In one tent, where one of the patients has been left, Agge counts a total of 624 pieces of shrapnel. The patient is alive. A piece of shrapnel about a centimeter across has pierced his sailcloth bed from beneath and stripped the skin from one of his ankles, then come to a stop in the bedframe. The shard is so sharp that it would serve as a razorblade, Agge writes. Now so many bombs are raining down from the sky that the number of unexploded devices makes it dangerous to walk along the busiest road in Elod, but the strangest bombings were just starting. *One can bomb people with paper too*, as Agge writes. In early May, Agge is brought a piece of paper that came down with the bombs, a page torn from a notebook with a message penciled in French that shocks him more than any of the planes' explosives, shrapnel, and mustard-gas bombs dropped on them during the preceding months. The letter states that the Italians are in Addis Ababa, where their government is now in control. From now onward, the other party in this war would be considered *illegal*, that is as bandits, terrorists (this amused Mara, *even back then*). The units of the Red Cross are henceforth instructed to contact the Italians. The letter ends with

effusive greetings complete with the name of a chief
lieutenant, presumably one of the pilots who only a
few days earlier was circling above the camp peering
out of the cockpit, examining the bushes for a man,
woman, child, or even an animal to kill. As though the
killers had lost their memory and now supplemented
their killing spree by pretending to be decent human
beings, simply for their own amusement. Now messages one more pompous than the other start falling
from the skies. *Peace, justice, civilization, welfare.*
Dissenters would be punished severely, and as if to
guarantee this, the letter mentions the Italian commander Rodolfo Graziani. It soon becomes apparent
that paper bombs are falling on other Red Cross and
missionary medical camps across southern Ethiopia.
Some of the letters posed questions and demanded
some kind of signal to the pilots, who promise to return the next day. The Swedes decide to try and flee
the country. They head southwest, the only direction
where they might avoid the Italians, if they are lucky.
The Swedes trade their redundant animals, sell their
hospital beds, and set off on a trek several weeks
long toward the Kenyan border and Nairobi, around
800km as the crow flies. Most of them have only light
clothes intended for the sweltering weather, but high
up on the plains the temperature plummets at night.
Every day they hear rumors about roads built by the
Italians, convoys of tanks, bandits organized by the

Italians, roaming Abyssinian soldiers, declarations of war between various European nations. Sweden is now at war with Italy, as are Germany and England. The situation is precarious, often dangerous. One evening, they are getting ready to spend the night in their tents outside a small hut. As evening draws in, they are shot at from the bushes, during the night shots fly across the hut. Tonight, no laws apply, says one of the locals to lighten the mood. In addition to all the difficulties they are expecting, during the expedition they almost lose all their documents too when a gang of criminals takes their mule, complete with its load. The materials contain hundreds of photographic negatives, among them images of mustard-gas victims, notes, diaries from the infirmary, pictures of individual people, Ethiopian civilians and their lives. *An ashen archive*, without which only the invader's words would remain valid, their peace, their justice, to say nothing of civilization and welfare, I thought as the Kungliga Biblioteket's caretaker rang a small bell to indicate that the building would be closing in fifteen minutes. The ashen archive talks about the normal, natural life that real bombs and paper bombs destroyed, *and it's from those ashes that the Ethiopian comes too*, I thought a moment later once I handed the book in at the returns counter and walked off toward Stureplan.

I was probably in a mood similar to what Mara must have experienced when he closed the book at the Swedish Institute and walked through the center of Rome to his apartment. The book tells us everything we need to know about the reality we see around us, said Mara, not because it is especially well written but because it illuminates matters that keep repeating. The books succeeds in doing this, though the author is simply trying to report what he saw and experienced, said Mara, and what I saw when I walked from the Institute, through the city center and along Corso, was exactly what Agge saw in Ethiopia, only transposed into a time of peace. Bertrand Russell, who was one of Wittgenstein's earliest supporters, wrote in the late 1930s about Mussolini's seventeen-year-old son who chuckled in the cockpit at the opportunity to burn hundreds if not thousands of Ethiopians to death, *hilarious, I'm sure*, said Mara. Russell used the boy as an example of the divine omnipotence at being able to kill people for fun and destroy everyday life from on high. Wandering through the center of Rome and looking around, one could see that same sense of indifference and omnipotence, he said. Mussolini's sons are five a penny round here, the very same little shitbirds with their bombs, and paper bombs these days too. I walked along Corso and watched the people out shopping. Now and then I found myself looking at someone's face, as though I'd noticed that they reminded me of so-and-so, someone of whom I had unpleasant memories. These people lived in a world where reality no longer sent them a bill, and never would, though in fact the bills that reality sends only get greater and greater, said Mara, and at that moment I realized there are more idiots here in Rome now than there were back in 1936.

As I walked through Stockholm city center that August evening, from the Kungliga Biblioteket to Stureplan, then hurried down to the corner of Regeringsgatan to buy a bottle of red wine and after that another block down the street to the grocery store at NK, I thought about what similar paths my life and Mara's life had taken. He moved to Rome; I did not, though years ago I had planned to do so. He was a rising star of the Finnish Wittgenstein school; I was not. He stopped doing philosophy; I did not, though I never got much further than the basics. But there were other things too, tens if not hundreds of things that linked our two lives, as I noticed, even now that I was in Stockholm and fed up with my noisy apartment in Enskededal, particularly the parquet renovation going on upstairs, every day I set off for the Kungliga Biblioteket and realized that I was following the path that Mara had shown me especially, to the extent that at the Hötorget metro station I walk

between the light-blue tiled walls and columns (*tåg
söderut, tåg västerut*) and into the exit corridor leading past Pressbyrå, a *kemtvätteri*, a *skomakare*, and a
nyckelservice and take the escalator up to street level
and the corner where Palme was murdered, which
Mara had shown me years ago when we walked past
the exact spot, after which he took me to the under-
pass running beneath Malmskillnadsgatan (year after
year, an old man stands there playing some kind of
stringed instrument with only two strings, he's always
in exactly the same spot, always wearing the same
dark-red fleece jacket and black polyester trousers)
and from there to the Kungliga Biblioteket, where
he showed me the reading rooms and encouraged
me to get myself a library card, though at the time
I was only visiting Stockholm for a couple of days.
We follow one another's paths like ants, as though
we are leaving tracks for those behind us to travel
along, I thought as I carried my groceries through
Sergel Square and headed for the metro station at
the corner of Åhléns department store, whose wood-
en walls always seem to exude a sense of homeliness.
We travel the paths that someone else has first shown
us and that we in turn show others, I thought. Now
Mara was in Rome as though chance had carried him

17   Swedish: "south-bound trains, west-bound trains."
18   A Swedish chain of newsagents; a dry cleaner; a cobbler; and
      a locksmith.

there, though in fact he was there primarily because I was supposed to move there first (he once said it was me who had given him the idea to move there in the first place). Our lives had taken such similar paths that it was frankly astonishing, I thought as I took the escalator in front of Åhléns and down into the metro station, and as the events Agge depicted in his book still echoed in my mind I noticed the way the murmur of conversation around me changed. People were no longer speaking Swedish now but Russian, Portuguese, Arabic and countless other languages I could barely identify. I realized that this had always happened, as I took this same escalator down into the subway every evening, Swedish at ground level, but in the metro carriages the blue seats and yellow handrails were the only things to remind us of that country. Every passenger has some kind of bag in their hand or slung over their shoulder. At Gamlastan station there are trains traveling in both directions on several different tracks, expectant-looking people on the wooden benches on the platforms, *tänk på avståndet mellan vagn och plattform*, after it stops [19] in Södermalm, the train crosses the Hammarby Canal, on the opposite shore is a windmill, *Restaurant Skanskvarn*, in the distance a row of yellow apartment blocks, from Gullmarsplan the train continues toward Farsta Strand, and by then most people on

19   Swedish: "mind the gap between the carriage and the platform."

their cell phones are speaking Arabic. It's only Arabs there, said Mara of the suburbs to the south of the city. Trees, woodlands, eight-floor apartment blocks on the hillside. *Nästa, Blåsut,* I get off the train, it's already dark. On the platform at Blåsut there are tripartite streetlamps and a modest wooden shelter painted white, beneath it a clock, wooden benches and round metallic trash cans, further off a beautiful pine tree stretches over the wire fence and into the airspace above the tracks. The train continues on its way, a few people remain on the platform, plodding their way toward the exit as another train glides into the station from the opposite direction. *Tåg mot T-Centralen*, in each of the train's illuminated windows sits a figure, a head and shoulders, dark, silent, traveling along a parallel path, all of them from somewhere in the south, perhaps even from the tiny village of Elod, above which Gunnar Agge spends his time watching the doves and keeping a lookout for approaching aircraft.

Mara had spent a few days in Rome trying in vain to find more information about Agge. All he could uncover was the year of his death, 1961. Ethiopia seems to have been the high point of Agge's life, after this

20 Swedish: "next stop: Blåsut."

21 Swedish: "trains toward T-Centralen [station]."

he disappeared from view and from all available databases, Mara explained as we stood up from the table at Casetta, bade the waiter farewell and, as soon
as we walked out of the gates, glared at the sharp-
nosed man still standing in front of Il Mulino, who
pretended not to see us, and perhaps he didn't. Agge
and Ethiopia reminded me of my aunt in Turku, as I
told Mara. In her final years, my aunt started talking
about *Somalis* and *immigrants* in irascible fashion.
Before that she had never said a crossed word about
the Somalis, but the more her health deteriorated
the more regularly she spoke about them as though
everything that caused her difficulty in life somehow
stemmed from the Horn of Africa. I visited her on
occasion, and whenever she started talking about her
illness, before long she was talking about the Somalis too. While she was sitting on the couch holding
forth about the Somalis, I looked at my surroundings, very little had changed over the years, in the
living room the couch was against the same wall as
always, even the throw was the same, the little trin-
kets positioned throughout the apartment were all in
the same places, my former room was the same, the
same bed, the same small 1950s bedside table. Long
ago I used to think that that room offered me asylum
of sorts, now I was very skeptical as to whether all
was well back then either. Years ago, I couldn't have
imagined my aunt ever uttering the sorts of things

she later said about the Somalis, just as I couldn't imagine it of my brother either. Years ago, my aunt was open to everything and everybody, almost curious, just as my brother used to know a lot of the immigrants in Kontula and had enjoyed their company. Back then, he still felt like he could keep up with the pace of life. Subsequently, he's faced a few setbacks, the kind everybody faces, but in addition to that something else happened, something in the country started to change, the sense of reality was changing, and my brother changed too, at the latest by the time he moved to Turku, to another apartment in the same block as my aunt, I was suddenly reminded. My aunt's vituperations about the Somalis all started when she had to step to avoid a Somali boy coming along the pavement on a skateboard, resulting in her stumbling into a drain half a meter deep and breaking her wrist, and since then all her ills have come from the Horn of Africa, though in fact she had already been diagnosed with cancer. When I was younger, I used to read the British empiricists at my aunt's place, thinkers who argued that we cannot know with any certainty whether the sun will rise the following morning, and now I wondered whether perhaps my aunt's scorn for the Somalis was in fact a botched attempt to talk about the uncertainty of tomorrow morning. The Somalis never do any work, they are *handed* money and given *home appliances* that they carry out to the trash, still in their unopened cardboard boxes, said my aunt. Once she became seriously ill, she began to live in a fantasy world. She didn't want to visit the health center, or to go for laboratory tests. *All the doctors are foreign.* I took care of paying my aunt's bills and noticed that she had cancelled her home insurance four years earlier, which was completely senseless. Eventually, I took out another policy and secretly paid it on her behalf. She didn't want to use a walker because she would have had to roll all the rugs out of the way. That's how she managed to bring down a Tynell lampshade that we were supposed to throw away. She broke a whole array of valuables in the apartment, Wirkkala glassware came crashing on the floor, and after this the living-room rug was full of tiny shards of glass. She destroyed untold amounts of Wirkkala glass simply because she refused to face facts and use a walker. As if the world were being destroyed one detail, one species at a time. Reality sends us bills, and we must respond with thought, but in life things take a different track, previous generations take out loans and leave them for future generations to pay off, and in all likelihood they have been taking out such great loans that now nobody is able to repay them. We arrive in a completely incapacitated world, yet we still imagine we can rely upon it, not to mention our incapacitated relatives, said Mara, *and that's the way the cookie crumbles.* Last summer, my mother told me I'd spent my first couple of months in an incubator, she'd slipped on an icy street and her waters broke. Mothers are like that, they can slap you in the face with anything, Mara chuckled. She'd mentioned the incubator before, but I had no idea I'd been there for months, he continued. In the days that followed, I had vivid recollections of how we used to joke about incubators when we were kids, they were *aquariums, greenhouses,* he said. Kids don't realize that life requires the right moisture and temperature or that a tiny baby born prematurely still needs the darkness of the womb, they don't understand what it means to a baby not to experience touch, because the skin of a premature baby hasn't fully developed yet. For many days, I wondered how I once had such an undue fascination for the beginning of life, our development and its biochemical premise. At the age of around thirteen or fourteen, I was in the habit of walking through the woods near Kontula, and in the autumn I would try to identify the constellations in the sky. Later on, I read endless amounts about the atmosphere, the clouds, the continents, light radiation coming from the stars, the speed at which the Earth spins and how all this together forms a system that is all too complicated for us to be able to predict or fathom, or even to call it a system. I read calculations about the oval shape of the Earth's

orbit and how even the slightest deviations from
that orbit would cause changes in living conditions
on the planet of a magnitude beyond our imagination. Or what incomprehensible repercussions would
occur if the Earth didn't have a moon or if the tides
seized up and one side of the planet roasted while
the other was frozen solid? Even indescribably small
changes would unsettle the biosphere that supports
life. The common understanding of a universe that
couldn't possibly be unsettled by some trifling matter
is completely erroneous, but people live their lives as
though nothing can unsettle anything, and to top it
all off, a few days after my mother told me about the
incubator, my thoughts kept returning to G.E. Moore
and to the fact that first thing in the morning I raised
my hand and looked out of the window at that small
woodland and felt an intense need to find my own
path into a shared reality and to investigate it, he said.

There was a hubbub all around us, tourists thronging past on both sides, somewhere was the aroma
of roasted chestnuts. Mara suggested we leave the
main drag. We turned into a gently sloping alleyway
where there weren't as many people. At the end of
the path, we climbed up a set of stone steps, in front
of us there was a church and a terrace giving a view
out across the city. We sat down on the steps in front
of the building. At least 30°C, I thought, and the

temperature was unlikely to drop much. Mara said something about Villa Lante, which was now *just around the corner.* He had managed to lure me to Lante, just as he had lured me to Rome in the first place. If it had been anybody else, I wouldn't have agreed under any circumstances, but when he asked, it really didn't matter whether I agreed or not. Here we are like two old herrings: when one turns, the other follows suit… We walked up the main thoroughfare at Gianicolo, trees stood tall on both sides of the road. It was late in the evening, but it was still unnaturally warm; cars, Vespas, and mopeds sped past us. I might not work in philosophy anymore, but this is still my world, I wouldn't be able to live in any other world, said Mara. He meant Lante. One always follows the same paths and never gets anywhere. One repeats the same things, making the same gaffes and mistakes again and again. The fact is, I don't like this city in the least, he said, but I need some Finnish company, and Lante is right here.

We arrived at the square with a view across the whole of Rome. Here and there people were leaning against the surrounding wall, and further off there were a few men who looked like immigrants, one of them gruffly hollering something down the hillside. There's a prison down there, said Mara, it's an old tradition that friends and relatives come up here to shout down to the prisoners, albeit more rarely these days because everyone has a cell phone. Hidden in among the trees were marble busts on plinths a meter tall, and when I mentioned them, Mara said there must be a thousand of those busts, then said something about Garibaldi. We walked across the square and the small park to the main gate at Villa Lante where Mara rang the buzzer, and just as the gate rattled shut behind us I realized what I was doing. It's easy to promise things, to agree to anything, but it's a wholly different matter to keep that promise, and as we stood in front of the building and waited for someone to open the door, it occurred to me that I shouldn't have come to Rome in the first place but should have stayed in Uukuniemi, there would have been loons and red-necked grebes out on the lake, I would have already heated up the sauna and would be about to bathe in its steam, or perhaps I would have finished bathing and would now be sitting enjoying the silence of the woods along the eastern border, as I'd been planning to do for months on this very evening, and the sense only grew when a young woman opened the door, greeted Mara, then scowled at me as if to ask *and who's this*, but left it to me to introduce myself. One is always so polite, even when one shouldn't be, I thought as I stepped into the foyer and extended my hand. The woman gave her name, told us she was on a stipend, asked what field my research was in and, without waiting for my response, began explaining to me (while some perfect strangers next to us stood listening) that I ought to *request* a residency here, and with a *decent* proposal I *might even get one*, she said in those exact words. I replied that I was *only passing through*, though she didn't seem to hear this and told us that she lived a short walk away from Lante. I said I wanted to see the views for which the villa's *loggia* was so famous, *without delay*, and walked through into the ostentatious *salone*, which was full of people, and after this onto the loggia itself, where there were even more people, and to my surprise, *it was just like in Uukuniemi.* The loggia was decorated with Midsummer birches, or rather with bunches of birch branches. I couldn't recall ever seeing birches in Rome, and though that evening I had thought about being back in the countryside, I'd forgotten it was Midsummer's Eve, and now I was trying my best to catch a glimpse of the famous view over Rome from behind a row of Finnish Midsummer birches. If I'd been in Uukuniemi, it would have been the one evening of the year when I might have heard voices and hullabaloo carrying through the forests, across the lakes. Here there was the atmosphere of a Finnish Midsummer, the same hullabaloo, only rather more restrained. Mara had found Annika and brought her to me. If we hadn't been in Rome, where simply being Finnish was enough to bring us together, Mara wouldn't have enjoyed himself as much as he

seemed to be enjoying himself now, I thought. Just
like at the department of philosophy, here he seemed
content simply at being allowed to be part of this. I
turned and made another attempt to push my way
to the window to admire the view, but as soon as the
grand urban panorama came into view, I noticed that
standing next to me was someone I knew from years
back, an ancient acquaintance, you could say, whom
I knew was a professor or adjunct professor somewhere or other. I greeted him. He gave a rather terse
response, and when a moment later I mentioned
my book just for something to say in reply to his
question about *what I'm up to these days*, he asked
what kind of book's that then? From his expression, I
could tell he was only pretending not to know and
was obviously satisfied at his feint. After this, he
seemed keen to show me I wasn't worth more than
a few words of his time and informed me that he
was going to the *artists' table over there*, by which he
meant a table where an acclaimed painter was sitting.

There and then I realized why I'd left philosophy
and why Mara had left philosophy too. If he hadn't
been so engrossed in conversation with Annika, I
would have tugged his sleeve and guided him toward
the door. Mara deals with situations like this far better than I do, I thought as I watched him from the
corner of my eye. He was standing a few meters away,
but I couldn't hear what he was saying. All I could

make out was the tone of the conversation; it was the tone of academic chit-chat, and I heard it all around me. At the artists' table, they were talking about whether all young writers in Finland try to write like Veijo Meri but fail. They all try to create a clear plot, full of twists and turns, and so on and so forth, the end of the discussion was drowned out by a group of student teachers standing next to me who, judging by their voices, were having a whale of a time. Indeed, it is specifically plot that prevents us from encountering reality, I thought. Once the noise had died down, conversation at the artists' table had turned to some painter or other, who somebody thought had done something of note, but my ancient acquaintance raised his hand, waved it in an artistic gesticulation, and said he'd *actually seen plenty of that lately*. Back in Kontula, when Mara used to start his mornings by raising his hand, he never waved his hand around to dismiss anything. He might have been in a world of his own and a little self-centered, but he never tried to belittle anything. Mara never tried to advance himself with conformist thoughts that had everybody nodding. He wouldn't have been capable of such thoughts even if he'd tried. He never tried to take the path of least resistance. He strove to

22

22 Veijo Meri (1928–2015), an acclaimed Finnish author known especially for his prose composed of short, laconic, 'modernist' sentences.

grasp reality, but even then, the luminaries gathered here would surely have said they'd *actually seen plenty of that lately*. I surreptitiously followed Mara and Annika's conversation, and I got the unpleasant sense that here Mara really was *allowed* to be part of all this. To me, he had always been an unrivalled thinker, regardless of what his own life was like. I turned again, this time heading to the window with greater determination, and noticed that the sky was full of swallows swooping here and there. I couldn't see what kind of swallows they were. I watched their nimble flight and recalled that until recently people believed that the common swift spent almost the whole fifteen to twenty years of its life on its wings, feasting on creatures living in the air, insects, aphids, spiders, hoverflies and gnats, they even mate in the air and gather everything they need from the skies. The old belief has it that the common swift also sleeps in the air, rising up to an altitude of two kilometers and letting the mass of air carry it along, like relaxing on a mattress. Loud conversation interrupted my thoughts; four men were standing behind me at the door to the loggia. Before I even got a good look at them, they gave the impression of being fit and brash, as though with only a single step the four of them had commandeered half of the loggia. Their arrival caught everybody's attention. I noticed that among them was an economist I knew rather well; we used

to be good friends fifteen years ago and our friendship was unaffected by the fact that we disagreed
about many things. He appeared surprised to see me
here. I told him the feeling seemed to be mutual. I
knew that he visited Italy a few times a year, though
never the south, not even Rome. He said he'd only
come down here to go running with his friends and
colleagues and that he'd be returning to the north
tomorrow morning. They all practiced endurance
running. He introduced me to the renowned re-
searcher I'd spotted in the group right away; the other two were engaged in loud conversation, and I
didn't recognize them. They all ran marathons, and I
learnt that despite the heat they had all just completed a 25km run. Their route had taken them through
the large parklands at Doria Pamphili and far out into
the countryside, he told me. The others started dis-
cussing whether there really was a turning point at
around 30km, by which they meant that moment in
a marathon, after around 30km of running, when the
glycogen in the working muscles has been used up
and the body starts burning fat, as someone claimed.
It's like *hitting a wall*, even the slightest incline is like
a wall in front of you. At precisely this point, the body
feels a chill, as though hailstones had suddenly started raining down, or you feel sick, or your back aches.
This is the moment when runners say they *hit the
wall*, the barrier, the hailstones, the dizziness. It's like

running on diesel, only the slow pumping of the muscles works, the pain in your quadriceps grows, your ankles twist, despair and thoughts of giving up fill your mind, then you push through this feeling of total exhaustion, I heard. One of the others said that hitting the wall is the sign of a bad training regime, though exhaustion is to be expected, of course. In endurance running, it's just the runner and his raw physicality, and in that moment he must assess the basic facts of existence. All four of them were talking about endurance running, their conversation punctuated with place names in Spain and Portugal where they went running during the winter months (I only recognized Los Pacos), the boys from the Finnish national team go running in the same places, one of them informed me, adding that *physical exertion* is normal, whereas sitting isn't normal. *Physical exertion* brings us closer to indisputable facts. *Physical exertion* dispels our learned, conformist behavior. Human beings aren't designed to *sit* but to struggle, to sweat and gasp for breath. Humans *need* physical exertion. In fact, physical exertion is our *calling*. Only physical exertion can release us from *the lazy man's* habits, the man asserts to some general chortling, though he seemed to be deadly serious and meant an experience of existence that is *charged with physicality*, he clarified. People cannot live without exertion; the body will reject us. Endurance fosters endurance, someone said, *humans are endurance machines*, the heart grows, engine displacement increases, we gain more capillaries, our muscle cells store more energy, running is a fundamental characteristic of our species while our sedentary culture in chairs and automobiles is a full-blown catastrophe. A passion for physical exertion pushes us toward goal-oriented running, not just jogging, the speaker chuckled. You start to enjoy the armpit abrasions, the muscle inflammations, the sprains. Only through hard, sustained exertion can we find our own weak spots, said the speaker, it might be a joint, a muscle, or the back, but it could also be the heart. Someone mentioned that, in most instances of a marathon runner's heart stopping, there is generally an underlying condition at play. Sudden heart failure is very rare, so rare in fact that we should be more concerned about people who don't run at all. Another one said that at the end of the day all people who take running seriously start dreaming or at least joking about how great it would be to die on a run, suddenly, painlessly. The conversation moved to Haile Gebrselassie and his running style, his left arm always bent, as a child he ran ten kilometers to school every morning, then in the afternoon another ten back home, his school books tucked under his left arm, and this extraordinary runner with multiple world records to his name still ran as though he was carrying a pile of books under

his arm. I remembered it too ... The Berlin marathon
in 2008, a sunny late-September day, *der kleine Mann
aus Äthiopien* positively *flying* along Französische   23
Straße toward the Brandenburg Gate where, thirty
meters above the ground, was a sculpture of the god-
dess of victory in a chariot pulled by four horses. In
comparison, the little man from Ethiopia looks like a
common swift gently gliding between the Doric pil-
lars, right through the middle, soon bursting through
the ribbon marking the finish line, he smiles, crouch-
es down, rests for a moment on his knees. *The whole
run came down to the last 12 km.* Every marathon
always comes down to the final 10 km, someone said,
the stretch after you've *hit the wall*. Someone recalled that the Ethiopians' success in running events
had begun here, at the Rome Olympics, and that it
was almost fifty years to the day since Abebe Bikila
took gold in the marathon that he ran *barefoot*. At
the time, people thought Bikila always ran barefoot
and must have always done so, but there are many
stories about why he decided to run without shoes at
the Rome Olympics, and now it's impossible to tell
fact from fiction. One of the stories said he'd read
research suggesting that if you're used to running
barefoot, the body's weight distribution shifts to the
middle or the ball of the foot, and then the foot is

23 German: "the little man from Ethiopia."

flexible, this is exactly how humans used to run when trying to exhaust small prey. The route of the Rome marathon started at Campidoglio and headed along Via Appia Antica, I learned. That's precisely where Mara had gone looking for the Ethiopian, I thought. A world-record-beating run, barefoot, Bikila was considered a country bumpkin who always ran barefoot. I thought of what Mara had said about Agge's book, even in Agge's day people laughed at the barefooted Ethiopians as their feet burned in grasslands poisoned with mustard gas. Before long, someone referenced hill running and exercises designed to increase oxygen uptake, capillary beds, and of course the levels of muscular glycogen, and again mentioned *physical exertion*, which perfectly suits the notion of *flying, running, or being an undocumented illegal, just like Mara's Ethiopian.*

It seemed the stipendiary had decided I was more an artistic than a scholarly guest, as she came and started talking to me in a friendly manner and wanted to show me the garden. Outside there was a small table with a few of the Villa regulars and a far greater group of people standing around it. *Tonight the noise and drinking will bring good wedding and cattle fortune for the rest of the year,* someone said, by which he obviously meant the old folk tradition, but nonetheless caused a volley of laughter around the table.

The bells at the basilica in Trastevere carried in from afar, followed only twenty or so meters away by a long holler coming from the square. I couldn't make out the language, but the holler sounded more African than Albanian or Romanian, who were five a penny in the city, and the tone of the cry suggested the hollerer was trying to get hold of someone in the window of one of the cells down below, until the sound was drowned out by laughter from the table. Someone had been telling an amusing story about a language gaffe and about what the waiter eventually brought to their dinner table. Out on the terrace, the hollers started up again, and again a new volley of laughter silenced him. This time, someone had gone into a department store and inadvertently asked for something hilarious. More volleys of laughter, then, from the square twenty or so meters away came an almighty cry as three of them hollered toward the prison in unison, but another howl of laughter and shrieking drowned them out, and as soon as the laughter and shrieking died down they hollered again, and again, still in unison, and at this my ancient acquaintance, whom I only now noticed was sitting at the end of the table, stood up, gestured to the others to lower their voices, raised a forefinger to his lips, tried to hush the others and indicated toward the square. Soon the last of those at the table stopped laughing, not a single glass or fork clinked, for a few seconds an unreal silence descended on the table, the cicadas chirped, the sounds of traffic could be heard along the riverbank down below, the bells at Trastevere had fallen silent, the air shimmered with the deep and distant hum of the metropolis. Everybody was waiting for these unknown hollerers to take advantage of the situation, but the seconds passed and nothing could be heard from the square, someone got bored, picked up a fork and pronged some cheese and olives onto a plate, until right next to us there came a wild, triple bellow, and when it stopped, there came a reply from the prison, a dark, solitary voice, perhaps a Somali, perhaps anyone from somewhere to the south, a voice that was relieved, comforted in the knowledge that these other people, whoever they were, were up there in the darkness hollering whatever it was they were hollering. Around the table, heads spun round to listen, expressions of feigned surprise spread across their faces, eyebrows rose, someone's hand and dessert fork pointed toward the hollerers, who had now established contact with whoever they were looking for. Someone took the opportunity to fill everybody's glasses, and my ancient acquaintance, who had called for silence at the end of the table, now decided to end it. He tapped the table three times, *inside*, he said loudly, then downed the contents of his glass in a single gulp. This caused a deserved volley of laughter, albeit somewhat deferential and more

subdued than before, and the conversation started
up again, this too more deferential than before, now
with an element of self-satisfaction that we had done
something to help these strangers, in fact, everything
that we could reasonably have done.

In the *salone* later that evening, once the endurance
runners had already left, someone started talking
about a flight to Finland, I'll be back in the countryside by tomorrow evening, I overheard the speaker
say. Here my thoughts give off sparks, but when I'm
chopping wood in the countryside those sparks return to my mind, he said. Here the sparks enter my
thoughts and in the countryside I can put them in
order, he repeated. When you're chopping wood at
the cottage in Finland, that's when you really understand what you've spent all winter doing here, someone else chimed in. When you've been at the cottage
for a fortnight and only been to the grocery store
once and haven't seen a soul in almost two weeks,
that's when you really understand this place... Here
it's impossible to get any sense of distance, he said.
Here it's impossible to understand, but when you're
chopping wood at the summer cottage, it all becomes perfectly clear. All around people leant closer
in keen expectation, but the speaker left his sentence
unfinished. That's why it's so refreshing to be here,
he continued, though it's refreshing to get back to

the summer cottage in Finland too. They provide the right kind of balance, Rome and the summer cottage, walking around Parainen and walking around here and sitting at a restaurant down in the square, eating pasta here and smoking a freshly snared pike at the cottage, or doing research here and chopping wood back home at the cottage, he said. My ancient acquaintance, who had been listening to the man for the last few moments, began by commenting that *we*, by which he presumably meant himself and his wife, *we* have been thinking about getting a second-hand log splitter, but there's something so satisfying about chopping your own firewood at the summer cottage that it's hard to give it up... You can get quite light-weight machines these days, it's easier to move the horizontal ones, and they're not even expensive... Even the smallest upright models can weigh 100kg, but the horizontal ones are lighter, around 50kg, no heavier, and then there are proper forestry machines that are as sturdy as anything... Soon, a man who had been standing listening, clearly a friend of my ancient acquaintance, said *chateaubriand* in a low, emphatic voice, though nobody around us seemed to gather whom or what he was referring to, perhaps dinner because he placed a palm on his stomach as

---

24 A predominantly Swedish-speaking island in the Turku archipela-
   go; a summer holiday destination popular among Finland-Swedes.

if to indicate that it was either full or empty, which in turn depended on whether the *chateaubriand* was already there or whether it was merely his intention, as I concluded, either he had already eaten the steak or the act of eating it was still in the planning stages, perhaps he was suggesting to the speaker that it was time to wind up his lecture and move to the barbecue outside. It was two o'clock, if not three, by the time Mara and I left, we walked back along the same street, the lawns outside lined with rows of busts. *Garibaldi's soldiers*, said Mara, there must be a thousand of them, and one of them was a Finn, though he couldn't remember where this particular bust was. Now there were only a few scattered wanderers in the square, the statue of Garibaldi on horseback in the middle, *a monument to all kinds of horseplay*, as Mara called it. We went through some of the evening's subjects and events, and once we got to the bottom of the hill, Mara stopped and told me he wouldn't come with me any further, he'd decided to *go and look for the Ethiopian right away.*

II
AND ONE

We have parallel lives…
— Maria

Everyone comes from Ethiopia…
— Gebre

Saturday afternoon, the red-and-grey bullet train is due to arrive at Napoli Centrale at 16:10.

From the moment I boarded the train, I've been reading Herling and thinking about that spring day at Uunisaari. The conflict had, as it were, *unsettled* my life, as I told Mara last night. My brother's life had taken one path, mine had taken another, but because he's my brother you imagine there must be some kind of family bond, yet our age gap only exacerbates the hope of any corrective steps. In fact, he's been on my mind every day since the spring, and it was only yesterday that I forgot about him for long stretches at a time, but today, now that I'm alone again, he has been with me since the early morning. The carriage is dim, curtains drawn across the windows, and when I pull them back a fraction, sunlight bursts through the windowpane. *Just look around a bit*, my brother said, and for a moment I try to imagine what the landscape might look like in his eyes. The people traveling around us are talking loudly on their cell phones, breezily informing others where the *freccia* is right now and when it is due to arrive. Sitting across the aisle from me, a boy of around ten years old is playing cards with his grandmother, his grandfather pulls out a lunchbox and a pen knife, starts slicing tomatoes and mozzarella, then burps as if to say *that's the way the cookie crumbles*, as Mara always said in these exact words, *in English*, having heard it from Jori Henrik and absolutely convinced that Jori Henrik must have heard it from Wittgenstein himself when he explained how to reach the point where philosophical problems dissolve of their own accord. Mara said he doesn't like Rome, but he does like Naples. The Neapolitans are the most *backward* people in Europe, he said, that's why he feels so *welcome*. If, instead of souvenirs, limoncello, and vintage grappa (which I wouldn't take my brother anyway, neither would he expect me to), I could show my brother the landscapes I was going to see, it might very well unsettle his life, I thought. Instead of the forests around Uukuniemi, I would see the landscape of Naples, which was Herling's landscape too. Whereas only a week ago, I'd thought I would take the boat and head to the island of Suitsa, tomorrow I would take a taxi and head to the *old places*, the earthquake epicenter to the north of the bay. I would look around, and perhaps the things I saw might give my brother some answers. Besides, the whole idea of the power of landscapes comes from Herling. Only a moment ago I'd read his assertion that the Yertsevo landscape had a healing effect on him. He even *medicated* himself by looking at it. Herling asserted that one of the aims of the gulag was to force the prisoners to believe that life at the camp was normal life, that no other form of reality existed, but on summer mornings, when the prisoners were marched to their worksites several kilometers away, the landscape opened up around them and reminded them that normal life was outside the camp, not inside. The prisoners who forgot this fact eventually cracked. On the rare occasions when these prisoners survived the camp, they were unable to leave and instead remained in the gulag doing odd-jobs or living nearby. As spring came and the weather began to change, Herling would stand beside the barbed-wire fence and gaze out at the landscapes beyond it, sometimes he even saw a figure in the distance, a human being, and he would imagine himself following that unknown person's footsteps, wondering where they were going.

Before the train arrives at its destination, I see two messages on my phone, both from Mara. It seems he had *stumbled* into the Ethiopian after all. It had happened in the early hours, soon after he and I had gone our separate ways. *You'll meet him*, Mara wrote, then said he was going to sleep and would be switching his phone off. By the time I boarded the train, it had been barely twelve hours since I'd bid him farewell. Last night, Mara said it would only be *a matter of time* until he found the Ethiopian, and it was a *miracle* that he hadn't already bumped into him, but Mara's determination was at odds with reality, I thought to myself, he and the Ethiopian had nothing in common save for a few topics of conversations and a bed, at best some shared fantasies for which reality would prove devious and unforgiving. All either of them had was what, as they say, people carry with them, and that is frighteningly little.

An hour later I step into my hotel room, two separate spaces with tall ceilings, bare stone walls, a feeling of elation at settling in. I unpack my bag and throw two of Herling's books onto the bed, the gulag book and the so-called *night journal*, or *Volcano and Miracle* as it is known, in which he wrote stories, essays, and catalogued daily events during the night for thirty years... It was as if I had entered the room with my brother and looked around it with him. When, soon afterwards, I started reading the *night journal*, I noted that it was almost as though Herling too had taken up the invitation to *look around* and so on, his gaze too seemed to be searching for something around him. The violence of the earth, Herling's *volcano*, begins to fuse with other catastrophes, or rather other catastrophes start to fuse with the volcano. To Herling, all catastrophes, large and small, shared and private, have a similar impact; they sever the bonds between people, their unique thoughts and emotions. In writing about the system at the labor camps, the interrogations and period of remand leading up to imprisonment, he says that the aim of this system is not simply to squeeze as much work out of the prisoner as possible but to split his persona apart, to tear gaps in his thought processes and logical associations, to derail the conveyor belts connecting past and present until thoughts and emotions are wrenched from their original moorings and left rattling against one another like disparate parts of a broken machine.

The title of Herling's book refers to the Bay of Naples, and here the eponymous miracle has a very specific task. It stops and reunites everything that the violence of the earth has torn asunder. It was here that bishops led groups of people brandishing religious relics in an attempt to stop the oncoming flow of lava, much like you and your friends march to the border with your blue-and-white Finnish flags, I might tell my brother... Compared to this, the Skjolden philosopher's attempt to trust in the wordless foundations of words stems from unshakeable ground, as though he were trying to repair a piece of broken machinery.

All things considered, Herling has rather little to say about miracles. When, having been transferred from the camp, he arrived in the Bay of Naples with Anders' Army in March 1944, Vesuvius duly erupted. At night, it glowed. During the day, ash rained down from a darkened grey sky. Villages were evacuated. A full twenty-six years later, having witnessed the gulag, Herling writes of those who lost their homes, saying that he *will never forget the faces of the inhab-itants.* He continues that anyone deciding to settle here, in the Bay of Naples, muſt have *an innate or acquired sense of the fragility of the earth and of human life.*

It was here, twenty years ago, that I put my marital crisis behind me, and it was here, three years later, that Mara finally put philosophy behind him. There's nowhere better to empty your head of philosophy, he said long afterwards, though when I was traveling toward the Bay of Naples with my then companion, who was putting the finishing touches to a long over-due dissertation along with several other scholars all putting the finishing touches to their long overdue dissertations, back in Finland Mara was ſtill a reg-ular gueſt of the prime miniſter at Keſäranta. I was clinging onto my marriage, which was as screwed as the Gulf of Mexico, as I put it to Mara laſt night. Everything I had heard about Naples in advance assured me that everything there was hurtling to-ward the abyss. Our *little group's* joint research topic examined the social consequences of the faċt that, over time, the continuous tremors on the north of the bay had made settlements there uninhabitable. To my surprise, Naples offered me reſpite for weeks and months, time to catch my breath, and later on Mara too recognized that same *miraculous* lifeſtyle in the very same place. He went as far as to say that *Naples is too much, even for Wittgenstein.* He had heard from Red-Cheek (this was the only anecdote in which Mara ever used Jori Henrik's nickname, he never used it otherwise, though in fact the name only ever expressed the greatest warmth), so, Mara had heard from Red-Cheek about how Wittgenstein's friend Piero Sraffa had shown him the *Neapolitan gest*, scuffing the fingertips along the skin under the chin, and wondered what might be this gesture's logical form — or grammar, as Ludde had told Jori Henrik — and this small gesture refuted all the notions that Wittgenstein had managed to put together on the Eastern front, and after this he simply had to return to philosophy. I don't know how much there was in Sraffa's gesture that needed *gutting*, but I noticed that whenever Mara told this story, he was moved to tears.

When I leave the hotel room in the early evening and head along a narrow street and up to the Spanish quarters, it feels as though I've hardly been away at all, I've just popped to the outhouse at Uukuniemi and returned a moment later. The streets are paved with dark slabs of lava, the soles of my feet recall the forms of the slabs, their worn smoothness. And there's something else *miraculous* hanging in the air, at every street corner, an inexplicable antidote to the stink of the sewers, a redeeming *miracolo* as per the title of Herling's book, though I can't quite imagine flocks of angels in the airspace above the city. It takes a moment before I realize it's Saturday, laundry day, the air is heavy with the combined smell of all the world's washing detergents, coming from thousands, indeed, tens of thousands of garments dangling on ropes hung across the streets.

At eight o'clock that evening, my brother would have heard a familiar-sounding complaint about *losing one's Heimat.*

Before leaving Uukuniemi, I had arranged to meet Maria at the bar at Gambrinus, which was a five-minute walk away for both of us. Maria is a friend from years back, who was in her home city visiting her sick mother. We usually meet up once or twice a year. She has lived in Germany for a long time, first in Munich then in Halle, and despite her family and tenured university position she said almost immediately *I have no Heimat anymore* and *I don't feel at home anywhere*, just as earlier in the spring in Uunisaari I'd heard that *Finland doesn't exist anymore...* Though I hadn't planned to, I tell Maria about the Ethiopian. *Mara was fixated on stumbling upon the Ethiopian. He went off to find him, at night, in the early hours*, I told her a few things I'd heard from Mara, and Maria's off-the-cuff response stayed with me. *Yes, we have parallel lives.*

Even before leaving, I had decided to ask Maria about her recollection of the Naples earthquake of 1980 and compare her experiences to what Herling had written about the very same event. She had already told me about it years ago, but I'd forgotten many of the details. I told her who Gustaw Herling was and that his writings had given me the idea that all catastrophes, both large and small and even private ones, have certain features in common. Maria knew I'd had some upheaval of my own in these parts many years ago and, in fact, she had even played a small but important role in the final stages of those events. She drives us out of the center for dinner, the traffic is as slow as it gets in this city at its worst. It is late, we find a random restaurant, in TripAdvisor language, *romantic, business meetings*. I tell the waiter we are in a hurry and ask whether we could have the starters and the mains together. *At this restaurant, everything is possible.* The food arrives almost at once, someone appears from the kitchen with a bowl of parmesan, for the pasta, *va be'*, and without asking proceeds to sprinkle liberal amounts of cheese on my beetroot gratin. It seems the bill was written in even greater haste, but the sums are duly corrected, and we leave. Ten or so minutes later, as we are walking back to the car, I feel an unpleasant sensation in my stomach just as I ask Maria to tell me about the earthquake. She was sixteen, had just met him, her future husband, as she put it. He has long since been a former husband too. The earthquake shook their relationship. *I couldn't trust him anymore.* They had gone to the cinema, the film began, then the rows of seats began to undulate, an earthquake. *He completely forgot about me*, said Maria, he *hurdled* across the seats toward the emergency exit *as though I didn't exist.* He would have left me there in the collapsing building, she chuckled. But the emergency exit was locked, and her future husband couldn't get out, everyone was trapped inside. A moment later, the door was forced open, and they saw each other. *He only remembered my existence once we were outside*, said Maria. The following nights, Maria's family did what thousands of other families did, they slept in their car at Piazza del Plebiscito, which was near their house and incidentally right next to Gambrinus. For months thereafter, she slept with the lights on and woke up many times during the night to stare at the ceiling. The quiet, slowly intensifying jingle of the chandelier is the first sign of another tremor, she says before we part company at the corner of Gambrinus.

The day's heat still hangs in the air, thick and monumental, my diaphragm feels tense, I turn and walk through the door and into Gambrinus. At the till, I pay for two limoncellos and settle myself at the bar. All the gold-rimmed mirrors are in exactly the same place as they were twenty years ago, the same Murano glass chandeliers hanging from the ceiling, the waiters are wearing the same uniforms, black gabardine, dark-brown striped silk waistcoat, white shirt, a golden-brown bow tie, the words Caffè Gambrinus embroidered on their chest in golden-brown thread, one of them is wearing a long apron, a *parannanza*, as I'd learnt long ago. I quickly drink my order, glance at the people around me. I go over what Maria told me, she'd said something important, something I was grasping for in my work on Herling back in Uukuniemi, but I couldn't bring the thought into focus, the fatigue and general weakness had taken their toll. A moment later, as I lie down in my hotel room, it feels as though there is a length of rough wood in my stomach. I go through the details of Maria's account of the earthquake, and as my stomach shows no signs of calming down, I decide to see what happened to Herling during the same earthquake.

On the evening of November 23, 1980, shortly after Maria and her future husband had gone to the cinema for the 7 P.M. showing, Herling goes to the bathroom to wash his hands. He gives the exact time as 7:35 P.M. The sound of running water is met with a second, grinding, rocky sound. The stone wall in front of him bulges, a bump appears in the bathroom ceiling. Herling feels as though he is staggering.

Another dizzy spell, just like in August, he thinks worriedly, he is consumed by a feeling he cannot put into words. It is not fear; as one who experienced the war and the gulag, he knows that fear always has a particular reason and that *somehow there is a way out*. This time, the feeling brings with it a certainty that there is no way out. It is *formless, implacable, and omnipresent*, closing his escape route in all directions, it is at once far away, outside him, yet at the same time *nearby* and *inside* him. The tremor strikes at his *primordial, elementary sense of his own existence* because he can no longer trust his senses. The sense of one's own existence is replaced with *a capricious force, blind, obscure, and unaware of its own power*, and yet, no matter how accurately these words might depict the events, they are only *words, words, words* that cannot describe anything. By the time Herling reaches the courtyard, dust is rising high into the air; toward Mergellina clouds of dust already *veil* the sky. In the street, Herling looks at the people's faces, everyone has the same expression, they are *terremotati*, a word related to earthquakes and denoting a face petrified with fear, *the expression of rubble*. Later on, people are dug out from under collapsed buildings. Their heads are indistinguishable from the rubble covering them, *man reduced to dust by the single blow of an unknown hand*. On the nights that followed, Maria's family, like so many others, slept in their car at Plebiscito. Herling stays at home. He sits awake, holding a *vigil* in his armchair, flicking through books. *Night seems to increase the dread of earthquake*, he writes in his *night journal*, and the fear of earthquakes *poses the ultimate questions with exceptional clarity and force*. I shift position, slide slightly further down the bed, and a rough plank of wood chafes against my innards. I get up, take a few steps, and have just reached the bathroom door when my diaphragm empties the contents of my stomach over the bathroom floor and tiled walls. There is vomit everywhere, even in the furthest corners of the room and the folds of the shower curtain. Cleaning up takes me over an hour, but when I finally get back to bed, I feel better.

After two hours' sleep, I wake and take the steps down to the small room where breakfast is served. *Ridiculous to come all the way out here to look around the old haunts. From now on I'm not touching anything except natural yoghurt.* Once an unfamiliar couple sitting in the other corner of the room get up and leave, I am the only person having breakfast. The family running the hotel is watching TV. The woman is Russian, her husband Italian, their child adopted from somewhere in Asia. The woman at the reception is Ethiopian, as I noted yesterday. My stomach is beginning to feel normal again and needs some food.

In front of me is a tray of fruit with plums, apples, peaches, kiwi and persimmon, but when I swallow a teaspoon-full of kiwi fruit, my diaphragm lurches and I run up the stairs to my room on the second floor. Once I reach the door, the key turns painfully slowly in the lock, and my digestive system doesn't care about any decisions I might have made regarding my diet, I clench my teeth together, but vomit bubbles through my nostrils, my mouth opens and I empty my stomach onto the floor in the hallway, multiple times. A moment later, the Ethiopian lady cleans up my mess while I try to wipe down my clothes. I tell her I must have eaten something that disagreed with me last night, and she nods, says she knows the problem *only too well*. This discreet manner comes so naturally to her that it wipes away my shame and humiliation. When she leaves, I lie down in bed and mentally go through yesterday's events. Maria and Herling have the same experience. A catastrophe can destroy people's mutual trust and empathy. Herling repeats this notion, no matter what he is writing about. Even natural disasters, if we can use such a word, do not unite people against a *common enemy*, that is, nature itself. The end result is always the same: the bonds tying people together are severed. In the gulag, this was done systematically. The amount of nutrition given to the prisoners was in direct correlation to the amount of work they did, and those at the camp were lured to work themselves to the bone for an extra paltry scrap of food. When they were working in groups and the food was divided accordingly, the system suppressed the prisoners' mutual empathy, the only natural bond that they could possibly have had when they were interacting with the guards. While toiling out in the forests, a weak or unskilled prisoner could expect no understanding from the others, *he was eating the others' bread*, and when the only chance of survival is measured in grams and morsels of bread, that meant he was simply *hastening the others' death*.

Big deal…? At the very least I should have managed to say this much from the end of the table in Uunisaari… because when people's mutual bonds are severed, they always try to tie them together again (that is, at least, on the better side of the barbed wire), and for that they need an external scapegoat.

Herling provided evidence that I could have shown to my brother, who would doubtless have scoffed another *big deal…* Reading the *night journal*, I noticed that Herling had visited the same areas north of the bay that I knew very well. He had visited Pozzuoli in the 1970s, in the early 1980s its old town was emptied and closed off, and I was there only a few years later. Twenty years ago, the former residents all had the same stories… My childhood home is up there…

High up on top of the hill is an abandoned town...
In 1969 the ground started to tremble, inching its
way higher... In 1982 it rose a full 160 cm... A single day might see several hundred little tremors...
The buildings, the harbor, tourism, everything...
The speakers, whoever they were, often gestured
with their hands, like flicking crumbs from a table...
Their memories usually ended by pointing to a small,
green-dappled mountain rising almost directly from
the shoreline... A row of beautiful small pine trees
stood along the flat ledge around the crater... The
mountain had risen up in a single night sometime
during the 16th century.

Herling wrote about his visit to Pozzuoli in the
spring of 1970, soon after the first mass exodus of
its inhabitants. Early one morning, a fisherman
had come ashore, having been at sea all night... He
doesn't even tether his boat to the quayside, but runs
instead to the town hall, his nets were full of dead
fish, *boiled* in fact... Of the town's 60,000-strong
population, half start packing up their belongings
and flee the town in fear of an undersea earthquake.
Soon afterwards, people said that bastard of a fisherman was lying, he was bribed, kept his nets in the
water goodness knows how long... If he was still here,
we'd split his head open... The assumption was that
people were intimidated out of their homes to make
way for real-estate speculators.

The people of Pozzuoli behaved the way people do the world over, they needed a culprit, a scapegoat, and when there were no immigrants to blame, even a local would do.

By around midday, I felt a little better and decided to carry on as I had planned and head to the northern shore of the bay. The only concession I granted my weakened state was a taxi ride from the corner of Gambrinus to take me the fifteen-kilometer journey.

I remember here and there seeing street corners between the monotonous blocks of flats, but when the taxi driver finally turns onto a road running along the coastline, I can already see the promontory in the distance and the *terra*, the old town, the houses one on top of the other like swallows' nests, the very place that was emptied and eventually closed thirty years ago. Now, five or six cranes stand tall above the closed city. The town should have been destroyed twenty years ago, and it was, and rendered uninhabitable once and for all. On closer inspection, I see that several of the houses have been renovated and painted yellow or wine-red, though they still don't look lived in. Behind them, most of the buildings in the *terra* are still dilapidated. I ask the driver to take me past the harbor and to the other side of the *terra*. I pay and step out of the car, which drives back along the same road we have just taken. In the harbor there are dozens of small fishing vessels, each with their own colorful parasol and blue-and-white striped awnings. There is nobody in sight. The *terra* rises up behind the harbor, but on this side there are nothing but ruins. The same inconsolable purposelessness as before, steps that don't lead anywhere, roofs that don't hold anything. I've been in this same place many times before. One day, I sat in the car in the shadow of these very same yellow-grey concrete bollards for hours, talking to my companion. Then, as now, looking at the panorama in front of me it was hard to comprehend that the earth moved, shook, trembled, that it was anything but a *terra firma*.

Here, Herling saw the destruction that can be wrought by nature and humans alike, something with which he was familiar from the snow-covered expanses of Yertsevo. Ultimately, it is hard to compare the catastrophes people face, Mara said only the day before yesterday. Twenty years ago, my companion and I were living a very normal life in Helsinki, yet still we were like the people Herling had described, people whose mutual bonds frayed and soon severed altogether, though what catastrophe had we actually faced?

In November 1989 a pack of wild dogs was running through the deserted train station at Pozzuoli. My companion took me to the house of an interviewee who lived in a recently built suburb. The family's sole breadwinner was a forty-three-year-old woman, a widow with seven children and who earned her living as a cleaner. I can't remember her face, only that her voice was like Anna Magnani's voice as she told us about the family's shared, short-lived holiday. For a year, the mother and children had put money aside every month to save enough so that the following summer they would all be able to visit Rome. The preparations for this trip had been meticulous, packed lunches made in advance, and in the nights leading up to their departure the children could scarcely contain their excitement. That morning, they set off for Naples, where the train was due to depart for Rome, and indeed it did depart, only without them. At the train station in Naples, they suddenly realized that the mother's wallet was gone, a pickpocket, their savings lost. There was nothing else for it but to take their packed lunches and return home. They too used to live in the *terra*, and they like all the other interviewees had all kind of curious notions about why the residents had been forced out of their homes. *They wanted the poor out of the way... Camorra wants the land... Fiat wants to buy the place and build hotels... It's all a NATO project...* Or simply a rub of the thumb against the forefinger and middle finger; whoever was behind it, it all came down to money. When someone steals your wallet at the train station, you can imagine the culprit. When people were swept from their own *terra*, nobody knew who was wielding the iron broom, but nobody believed it was because the earth was trembling. Now people lived in trailers at the foot of the *terra*, a new residential area had sprung up only five kilometers away. If the ground trembles here, it will tremble a stone's throw away too. Or even five kilometers away. *It's always the lives and property of the little people that end up being gambled away.*

When, having been taken prisoner by the Red Army, Herling eventually signed a fake confession drawn up by his interrogators in which he admitted attempting to cross the Lithuanian border in order to fight against the Soviet Union, he became a criminal and soon found himself on his way to the gulag. He and a Polish companion, a fellow prisoner whom he had met in captivity, were sitting on a train in one of Stolypin's carriages, that is, a former cattle wagon, on the lower berth where his companion had laid out his warm coat. On the upper berth, three common criminals were playing cards. One claimed to have been given fifteen years after an incident at the Pehora camp when he had taken an axe to one of the cooks who had refused to give him an extra serving of barley. Herling forces himself to laugh. Snow, forest. Soon, the same criminal throws the cards from his hand, hops down from the berth and stands in front of Herling's companion: *Give me that coat, I've lost it at cards.* The companion opens his eyes, doesn't answer. *Give it to me, or I'll...* The criminal is holding his forefinger and middle finger apart, a gesture signifying the convicts' method of killing people at the camp by thrusting their fingers into the victim's eye sockets. The Polish companion stands up and surrenders his coat. Herling learns that in card games the criminal convicts would often stake whatever somebody else has to hand. Whoever loses the game has to procure the item from the other person. And Herling soon learnt that, in the early days of the labor camp in 1937, even a bystander's life could be used as a wager. A political prisoner sitting in the corner of the barracks would have no idea that the greasy cards slapping against the bench might in fact seal his fate.

This is an economy, in its most primitive form. In Pozzuoli, everyone was convinced that, one way or another, they were all sitting in one of Stolypin's cattle wagons like underdogs, pawns, wagers.

January, a sunny day... a municipal worker took us on a tour of the shuttered city. A down-to-earth guy in a brown suede jacket, a hardy face, a sprawling moustache, no-nonsense conversation. Over the last fifteen or so years (after most people had left the city, I assumed), plants had occupied the streets, captured the walls, the gables, and crept their way into old apartments. The windowpanes were smashed, the gutters collapsed. Our route wound its way in and out of the houses, most of them without a roof, rising and falling one story at a time. Broken Coca-Cola bottles in the corners of the rooms, walls covered in faded posters of singers who hadn't recorded a note since the 1970s. Inside the church, the gilding had been torn from the fixtures. Here and there lay items of furniture, forgotten and left to the mercy of the elements, individual kitchen appliances, tables, chairs, vinyl and cassette players, shoes, winter clothes and so on. From the edge of the city wall, you could see down into a gravel pit with trailers, the former residents of the *terra* living there. A mild, sunny day. At the foot of the wall was the small center of the town, where people lived as though the ruins weren't there at all. *You forget about it… You learn to close your eyes…* The small potted plants standing by the trailer doors were shabby; they reminded me of the worn-out old shell suits and cheap baseball caps, the woolen sweaters, the track suits, the tired and swollen faces, the gaunt cheeks, the puffing on cigarettes. Uncouth voices all around, harsh cries, laughter, shouting, sighs whistling between missing teeth. The middle-aged and older women were so overweight that it must have taken them considerable effort. The girls' large round or triangular earrings scraped against their necks when they turned their heads.

Thick, black hair. *Salve, salve.* They had been driven from their homes *like cattle. My home used to be up there.* All this in a shrill, rough voice, a curious mixture of innocence and directness. They were *Bethlehem's cattle*, someone said. The women's jumpers had heart-shaped patterns on them. Between the trailers, long wooden poles held a row of plastic awnings in place, like a continuation of the endless lattice of scaffolding holding up the walls and masonry across the street. A suitable place for our perfectly average life twenty years ago, its sheer inanity, I thought now. In our first serious relationship, we always repeat the worst aspects of our childhood homes, Mara told me once. The conformism we glean from our surroundings is like Herling's depiction of *the unknown hand, the power unaware of its own majesty, to which we learn to close our eyes.* My brother would have said that the greatest conformism of all was *not thinking further than your own arse*, and even in Kontula you might hear someone say that so-and-so's world *only reached as far as his arse could drag him.*

An hour later I find myself in the place where the road leads us to the dead, or so people used to believe. I've been walking, or perhaps it would be more appropriate to say I've been shuffling in a circle around an enormous flat crater with small islets of woodland, laurel trees, holm oaks, sage and gorse; behind the woodland there was a large plateau covered in volcanic ash where the whiteness of the earth was dazzling, the air stank of sulfur, the heat and the horseflies wouldn't give me a moment's peace, smoke rose from fissures in the ground and curled its way up the steep embankment further off. I felt weak, and when I saw a wooden bench in the shade of the trees I lay down, closed my eyes and wedged my wallet against the back of the bench in case I fell asleep. Behind the nearby trees, there were a number of dome tents, old camper vans, a few shacks selling things, a campsite, *only eastern Europeans*, I concluded from the voices. There was nobody in sight. In ancient times, people believed that a road ran through this place leading underground to the homes of the dead.

The taxi ride from the harbor to the *Vulcano solfatara* took only five minutes, but I didn't have the energy to walk. In front of a small arched doorway, the elderly tout at a nearby bar watched my arrival, launched into his usual spiel, pointed at the patio; his tone was friendly, so I stood there and exchanged a few words with him. *Food poisoning*, I said. *Drugs, medicine, injection*, he replied and mimed injecting himself in the forearm. Along the bar's wall was a long table, volcanic rocks, lava, coral, pearls, cameo brooches, all intended as souvenirs. I ordered a Diet Coke, but before it was brought to the table, I felt sick and had to get up. The toilet cubicle was cramped and dirty. Endless amounts of hand washing. I leant over, stuck my fingers down my throat, and only then saw something deeply unpleasant. At a moment like this, the last thing you want to see is human feces. I washed the toilet bowl, rewashed my hands, stuck two fingers deep down my throat and emptied the contents of my stomach. Another round of hand washing, after which I staggered across the bar, drank my Diet Coke, and set off for the crater.

Herling had taught me that wherever there is a road from which nobody ever returns, somewhere nearby there must be a sauna. In the middle of the sweltering crater, the sauna is a simple brick construction with two closet-like alcoves built into the wall where you can lie down and curl up. A small sign explained that in one of them the temperature is 60°C and in the other 90°C. Next to them, above a pile of yellow sulfuric rocks, the temperature was 160°C, but the higher the temperature the more the horseflies felt at home. Another sign explained that the crater was fitted with corner reflectors to observe seismological activity.

I drift off, unsure whether I am more asleep than awake, I can hear people's voices, but there is nobody in sight, the air shimmers with smoke, the stagnant baking heat, the sun haze.

There on the bench I chuckle, half aloud. As though shadows had appeared from amid the smoke and the glare. The voices had disappeared, and now I felt alone in the crater, as if left inside a deserted theater. Here wanderers chosen by fate can meet one another, people who by dint of their societal and economic differences would never have crossed paths while they were alive. Here amid the stench of filth, the rich can appeal to the ferryman, demand postponement for a fee and ask to take all their worldly belongings with them, while the poor, already used to subservience, will supinely give up their seat to anyone who asks, and even take up the oars or the bail if ordered to do so. There can be no return, so while for one person this could be the final struggle, for another it is merely business as usual, political horse-trading... *This team will get some real results... An affable chap will do just fine... All things in good company...* Vanity flourished, and even if someone was concerned about the future, be it underground or in the skies above, nobody seriously believed they would be forced to leave everything behind, a bodybuilder his muscles, a rich man his arrogance, a philosopher his convoluted notions... *It is like pressing the door shut behind oneself*, said Björling shortly before his death. Wittgenstein, when he heard that the end was drawing near, sighed simply *finally*, or so Mara always claimed... The depiction and mood could equally apply to the moment when Herling arrived at the prison camp that dark evening in the middle of winter and saw the observation posts in the distance, like *four crow's nests placed high on wooden stilts.*

There on the bench, half-asleep, I wondered why Mara had talked about the Ethiopian so insistently, as if this man had always been one of the recurring topics on our walks around Kaivopuisto. When Björling commented on his approaching death, that it is like pressing the door shut behind oneself, he wasn't telling the truth. Even Wittgenstein's *finally* sounded a little hollow. One way or another, humans always try to resist loneliness and crow's nests. A few brief trysts notwithstanding, Björling's sexual life was lonely, and Wittgenstein's wasn't much better. Herling too told us something about loneliness when he described how the convicts systematically hunted down and raped any women who arrived at the camp. It was part of the camp's economy: scraps of bread, a rape, felling a tree, like twisting a branch from a pine, a handful of berries from a sprig.

Mara searched for the Ethiopian as though this was a form of *survival*, morning upon morning. Later that afternoon, Mara called, twice, and said that the Ethiopian was here now. I didn't ask whether *here* meant at Mara's apartment or the fact that this relative stranger had now been located. They had done

simple things together, strolled, chatted, gone grocery shopping, cooked some pasta. It sounded almost
like two people's shared loneliness, or the tranquility
of Skjolden when compared to the folly of the world,
which I encountered later that evening when, with
considerable exertion, I stood up from the bench and
shuffled back to the arched doorway and the Solfatara office. Two old men were sitting in the middle
of the room. Their thinning white hair and beards
were scruffy, behind them were a few large potted
plants, old bookcases, dark wood, glass doors, scien-
tific-looking books and tomes published sometime
between 1900 and 1910. In front of the men was a
bulletin board showing clippings and articles dating
from March 2009 and cut from American and Italian
newspapers. *Solfatara compared to Viagra*, the head-
lines declared. In the tissues of the male member,
two enzymes had been discovered which together
produced hydrogen sulfide, and this in turn caused
an erection and the enlarging of the blood vessels.
Natural Viagra, the same gases as in the *Solfatara
shrouds*, the devil's issue... I take a moment's rest on
a chair in the office and ask whether the ground still
trembles almost daily... It's been quiet for the last
fifteen years, the ground making only small motions
back and forth, chuckles one of the men, suggestive-
ly rocking his fist back and forth a few centimeters
at a time. Always the same old jokes... *The pot isn't*

simmering... The giant isn't smoking... There's no caul-dron quite like it... This is a VEI 8-category *caldera*, a supervolcano, he laughed. Fish in the sea could be boiled alive at any moment... Then the bubbling will bring them up to the surface like great white fillets on a restaurant plate... Some kind of eruption is im-minent, that much is clear.

Back in my hotel room later that evening, the day's exertions collapse into bed with me, and it takes a moment before I have the energy to take my tem-perature. It's 38.4°C. I drift off to sleep and wake up during the night, not hungry, though I haven't eaten all day. I am half asleep, half awake, for a while I can't remember where I am, but I feel a little better and switch on the reading lamp. Twenty years ago, I used to look at these same places from one week to the next, but as I start flicking through the brochures I bought from the old boys at the Solfatara and think back to our *little group's* lies and decades-old deceits, it occurs to me that I never really *saw* anything. I study a historical engraving of a group of aristocrats who long ago traveled from far away in the north to admire the lava flows... Horse-drawn carriages, plat-forms, sedan chairs, women in long skirts, hats and diadems on their heads, there's a man sitting on a deckchair sketching the panorama, a young man and woman, perhaps looking for a way to elope together, they have walked out to the furthest safe ledges in the distance, the man is standing in front showing the woman the lava flows... We were like that too: idle, cruel, stupid. Standing in front of a raging inferno we imagine that at most we will burn our nose, our toe, or little finger, the belief in our own exceptionalism is so unshakable that there's no way a disaster affecting the *hoi polloi* could ever befall us.

I wished Mara could have been there with me to comment on the image, chortling upon seeing something that could easily apply to our time too, just like he did that summer when I walked across the yard to his place almost every day, my brother was seven years old, but he too spent his time in and around that same yard, always appearing with his bike at some point during the day. Mara had a habit of always telling me about what he'd been reading that morning, laughing as he explained how a particular section should be understood. After this, he put his books aside and forced me to listen as he played his flute. He played straight from the score, stopped, furrowed his brow, leant closer to the music, then continued his painfully pedantic reading of Bach's counterpoint until he stumbled in the exact same spot again... There in my hotel room, floored by the heat, I imagined I could hear his stumbling flute as I read about how Monte nuovo, the green-dappled mountain on the shores of Pozzuoli, rose up from the earth in a single night, Mara stumbled and chortled, and out in the yard my brother was living his seven-year-old life, he too stumbling on his bike and chortling, fumbling his way onward like the tentative notes of the flute. At around midday, the earth at the shores of Pozzuoli rose five meters, I read, and the flute stumbled again. The sea retreated hundreds of meters from the shoreline, forming sandbanks and shallow pools, the sun glinted against the flanks of the thousands of thrashing fish that the locals rushed to gather up. People lay claim to everything revealed by the departing sea, even the court turned up to divide the land, not only to its favorites, but into taxable property. An hour or two after sunset, a molten rock the size of a bull was spat up into the air from the bowels of the earth, contemporary witnesses attested. A great fissure appeared, tearing the land apart at the seams. Loud noises filled the air. The earth vomited smoke, fire, rock and a silt of thick ash. Sulfurous compounds and fumes issued all around. The birds and animals were covered in yellow sulfuric ash and died or let people capture them with their bare hands. Soon afterwards, ash covered the streets of Naples too, blackening the palace façades and tarnishing their beauty. Everyone who'd had the chance to leave had already done so, but now, at night, the poorer inhabitants of Pozzuoli headed off to Naples on foot, carrying their children and scant possessions in their arms. Some were carrying birds covered in ash, others the fish they had plucked from the shore. Many wore nothing but a shirt, some had run out into the night stark naked. *Their faces were painted in the colors of death*, wrote one contemporary witness. In Kontula, sixteen-year-old Mara's Bach kept stumbling at the same spot, like so many human endeavors. If Mara had been reading this with me, he would have laughed and cried, just like he used to back in Kontula, and there in the dim of the hotel room I thought that, if only I could make my brother laugh and cry too, it might very well unsettle his life. In Pozzuoli, people's curiosity soon conquered their dismay at the natural disaster. The viceroy and his entourage rode out to the spot, or as near as it was possible to go. The earth was covered in a layer of ash half a meter thick, columns of smoke obscured the sky, the terrain was like a churned field. Word had it that beneath all the smoke there was a mountain the size of Vesuvius. The viceroy was thinking of profit, the people were there for the spectacle. The mountain was by the shore, so many curious onlookers arrived by boat and climbed up the hillside all the way to the edge of the crater, heedless of the ash and the fact that the soles of their shoes were left singed. From the crater rim, they could see down into the cauldron with water boiling deep at the bottom. The mountain was 134 m tall and had risen in less than twelve hours. An average of one meter every five minutes, I calculated. The following Sunday, when several dozen or perhaps more than a hundred curious souls had gathered at the summit to behold the newest local attraction, an eruption shook the crater and belched up a cloud of red-hot ash that came rolling down the southern face of the mountain. Many onlookers were consumed in the flames, toppled over by falling rocks, or overcome by the smoke.

Two days later I view the panorama of Pozzuoli from far out at sea, from behind the window of a hydrofoil. At the far end of the bay, the cranes at Pozzuoli gleam in the sunshine. Standing dozens of meters tall at the end of the peninsula, the rock faces show horizontal layers of sediment, *ash beds*, as one of the men at the office called them. I have already accepted the thought that I failed to show my brother these places. He would have responded to everything just as he did in Uunisaari, *big deal.*

Ten or so minutes later, the vessel arrives at the island of Procida, situated at the furthest edge of the caldera. On the quayside the heat is almost supernatural, it throbs in my head, flickers in my eyes and triggers an animalistic yearning for something salty. In heat like this, it is easy to envisage fish boiled alive, the hand of an unknown chef throwing them up into the tangle of ropes, fishing nets folded on wooden crates, rough tarpaulins, thick hemp ropes, waste bins and oil cloths dotting the quayside.

As we were arriving, from my vantage point out at sea I'd looked at a building rising up from the local *terra* and towering above the water and the hundred-meter cliff. Rows of empty windows, one on top of the other, bushes wherever there was even the smallest patch of horizontal space. The enormous complex was a prison, abandoned since 1988. My pocket-sized travel guide claims that nowhere else is there such a magnificent vista over the caldera and the entire Bay of Naples. Later on, the cliff and the prison reminded me of the Elod caldera and Agge on his mountainside, though I couldn't get in through the rusty metal grate at the front of the prison, the whole place was closed, through a small peephole one could see the wild greenery, leaves, branches, pieces of corrugated iron, collapsed gutters and ornate gables, peeling paintwork, as though time itself lay rusting, incarcerated. Since there was no entrance, I turned back without knowing what to do. The heat was still unbearable, and after roaming around for a moment I saw a couple of people disappearing into a narrow gulley between two houses, I followed them, and at the end of the gulley I stepped into a small lobby-like office where a talkative lady was explaining that the place used to be the church's such-and-such and had been hewn into the rockface on several floors.

A world of miracles, the walls of the narrow corridors were lined with glass cabinets, their shelves showing paintings that local fishermen had commissioned after being rescued from a shipwreck or some other disaster. In one of the paintings I recognized the island of Procida, at the top of the painting was the *terra*, in the foreground a bleeding fisherman was being carried ashore from his boat. Next to this were paintings depicting shipwrecks, all of them bearing an amateurish illustration of the Virgin Mary and the letters VFGA, *voto fatto grazia avuta, vow performed grace received.* On red-velvet display cushions there were silver hands, arms, a full-length portrait of a woman in a traditional skirt, another full-length portrait, this time with only a loincloth tied loosely around the hips, somewhere the initialism VFGA, then more stomachs, chests, hearts, arms, eyes, feet. All brought here because someone had been rescued from a disaster, from nature's unpredictability, or someone's health had been saved, hence the body parts and the VFGAs, but as I turn around in the corridor, I am startled. There is a familiar face on the wall. One of the glass cabinets contains several black-and-white photographs of Marshal Rodolfo Graziani, the man behind the bombing of Agge and Hylander's camps. Graziani, right here above the ash beds, which began to assume new, literal significance in my mind. Behind the glass, set against the dark wall paneling, are four black-and-white photographs and a fifth that is either a press clipping or a photocopy, all displaying Graziani's familiar stony features. Next to them, some yellowing photocopies of the covers of Graziani's books, their title pages, dedications and letters to Don Luigi Fasanaro, the director of this very institution, all written during Graziani's indictment in the late 1940s. In these letters, Graziani explains how excellently he has enjoyed himself here, *nel dolce di Procida*, as he rounds off one of his dedications. Graziani was here on the island awaiting trial where he was ultimately sentenced to nineteen years' imprisonment, though this was merely an attempt to prevent his extradition for war crimes, and he was released after serving only a few months. Now, not only Graziani but the previous few days, the ash beds, the earthquakes, everything I had seen along the northern shores of the bay, all this formed a path to Mara's Ethiopian, a link. *We have parallel lives*, Maria had said a few days ago. Even the lives of people who at first glance have nothing to do with one another can cross paths and intersect with one another, and now the *old places* and my personal memories were intersecting with the life of this unknown man. Graziani had promised to conquer Ethiopia with or without the Ethiopians. After the military

25

25   Italian: "in the sweet bosom of Procida."

campaign, he was appointed the Marquis of Neghelli. It was to this same settlement, still modest to this day, that Gunnar Lundström, driver of the Swedish expedition, drove from Hylander's camp to fetch medication, and after loading up his truck drove all the way back again without delay. Lundström with his prominent jawline, squinting as he posed for the camera in a photograph taken merely four weeks earlier. After the exertion of the drive, he slept for four hours in the cab of his truck. Then, during morning prayers, a piece of shrapnel from an Italian bomb sliced off part of his jaw and he was driven back to Negele, now unable to speak. Lundström died before arrival at Negele, where he was duly buried. Graziani would doubtless never have heard of this Swedish stranger, and if Lundström knew anything about Graziani, probably nothing more than his name.

You'll meet him...

In the morning, just as I am standing on the platform waiting for the train to take me back to Rome, Mara calls. He is *out and about* with the Ethiopian. He asks me to call him when the train reaches Termini... *Yes, he's right here next to me.* The platform smells of diesel and detergent, further ahead the stagnant air shimmers above the tracks as though it is about to burst into flame... *I'll explain later... and hi, by the way.*

Two hours later I stare out of the metro window at a former industrial area and its steel structures, like giant grain silos or watchtowers, I think, behind them is the place where Mara walked along the riverbank. Following his instructions, I get off at EUR Palasport, a dozen or so kilometers south of the city center. *This could be Germany or somewhere in Scandinavia.* Standing across the street from the metro station is a colossal 1980s office block some twenty-plus floors high. A broad thoroughfare runs through the area, traffic flowing in several lanes in both directions, I am the only pedestrian, between the grass, the sturdy trees, the shrubs and the lanes of cars there is a walkway barely half a meter across. On both sides of the highway, the 1980s building stock modulates into fascist-era architecture so seamlessly that one barely notices the change, except there is perhaps something in the scale of the buildings and columned corridors, the tuff, the limestone and marble, something more humane than the steel behemoths of forty years later (the rows of balconies running along the fourteen-story towers soon reminded me of the Caproni bombers). The central square is easy to find, in the distance, at the other side of the square rising gently to one side, is Mara's familiar figure, and alongside him another, this must be the Ethiopian, both sitting on the steps in front of a building standing over twenty floors high.

As they stand up, the scale of the buildings and the square around them is so grand that it gives the impression of an existence from which all elements of daily life have been removed, as though we were surrounded by the expansive, barren Lappish landscape, I think as I look at the two figures. The Ethiopian is pushing a bicycle, and I can see from afar that he is wearing the blue-and-red Lindeberg shirt that Mara bought at Stockmann's years ago, a winter shirt in this heat.

Salve, salve... the Ethiopian looks a little over twenty. Right from the start, he gives a pleasant impression. His handshake is firm, his face is open and receptive (or expectant and timid), his eyes moist, his irises wide. He is pushing a blue women's bike, *a Swedish bike, Pilen, three gears.* His voice is dark, rising up to a falsetto when he laughs, a curious contrast to his muscular frame. Though his demeanor is meek, there is a very physical presence about him. Judging by his appearance, he could be a local, or Portuguese perhaps, or a Turk from Germany. He could have spent his childhood in a suburban apartment block nearby, lived his entire life at the same address. I assumed he must have arrived in the country only recently, but it turns out he has been here for a while, perhaps a year or two. *Two months, four months, six months, two weeks*, the weeks and months punctuate his speech as he talks about finding an apartment, *brushing up* his Italian, getting a bike of his own. Everyone is in a hurry, *tempo tempo*. His life is full of schedules, I comment, and he responds with a smile, *yes, if you want to get somewhere, you must have a schedule, without a schedule...* He draws his fingertips across his throat and laughs, pulls a brown paper bag out of his satchel and offers us walnuts as I turn to Mara and say *so this is the one who gave you the what the hell is it in Finnish*, but Mara brushes my words away with a flick of the hand, as if to say the matter is now closed.

The Ethiopian speaks rather little, mostly just inter-jecting with *yes, andare, va be', since the morning.* Kurre (if not Swedish Gurre, indeed; I wondered whether Mara had had something to do with this nickname, but later that afternoon I learnt that the name had existed long before the encounter with Mara and was a derivation of his Christian name, which was Gebre or Gebru, at first I couldn't make out which) said they had been out and about since the early morning. Gebre (or Kurre) had been kicked out of his lodgings, his friend's apartment would be empty for a few weeks, and now he had to pick up the keys, that's why Mara had asked me to get off at EUR. This was the *explanation* Mara had promised

26

26   Italian: "moving, right."

that morning, and this is why we were here. Mara suggested that we walk to a park a few blocks away. On the way we chatted, asking the kind of things one asks in a situation like this. The park was behind a world-famous building, I recognized it from photographs. On each side of the building there are nine arcadian arches on six floors, making the whole construction look like a giant dice. Mara tells me that Kurre (as Mara calls him) has moved twice in the last month, and that's why he is only carrying the essentials, a bike and the grey satchel that Gebre (as I now find myself calling him) taps with a smile as Mara translates what he just told me in Finnish. *It's normal, tempo di andare avanti.* Gebre speaks good, if rather stumbling English and excellent Italian. Once in the park, we cannot find a bench in the shade and instead sit on the grass under the trees. Gebre passes the bag of walnuts around. When his phone rings, he leaves the walnuts with us, grips the handlebar of his bike and says *fifteen minutes, twenty minutes.*

He's alright, I say, and Mara nods. Soon afterwards, he adds that Kurre is all smiles, but he can get a bit violent. Whenever he manages to borrow some money, he spends it straight away on food and, in particular, drink, and the more he drinks the more troublesome he gets. If a random passer-by says so

27

---

27 Italian: "time to move on."

much as a crossed word to him, he could do anything. One wrong word and he flies into a rage with
me too, he kicks and punches and is just completely
impossible, and the most irritating thing is that he
expects me to save him whenever he's in the shit, and
when that happens once or twice, the next time he
demands the same again, only to the power of two
or three, which is understandable of course because
he needs help, but whenever he suggests going for
a few drinks, he ends up having an argument with
people in the street and eventually with me too, said
Mara. Well, there's another side to him too, he's really
direct and sincere, he's just desperate for some affec-
tion, and he's completely screwed, I've never seen
anyone sweat like he does while he's asleep, the sweat
genuinely drips out of him onto the sheets.

Fifteen minutes later Gebre comes back, lets his bike
fall to the grass and sits down with us. There are
beads of sweat on his forehead; he's been pedaling
hard though it's probably 35°C.

He is in boisterous spirits, and at first the subject
of his laughter is the locals (he giggles and slaps his
hand against his thigh): if an Italian stops to talk to
another Italian, they're either looking for money or
sex, there are no other options... And as for the Germans, always walking the family cat or dog, chatting
away to it as if it understands... He rolled over on the

grass, the corners of his mouth ready to rise in laughter, but it seemed as though something was bothering him, plaguing him, he was nervously tossing around as though in bed and his constant chuckling was an attempt to avoid something that was about to catch up with him.

We have been sitting in the park for around an hour when the exhaustion hits me. I nod and occasionally mumble something in response ... The bees are buzzing, traffic hums in the distance. A moment later, Gebre breaks the silence, asks whether I know what a ... *dablin, dabbler* ... is, I can't make out the word, I've noticed he stammers at times, then eventually I realize he's trying to say the word *Dubliner*, which makes me think of James Joyce but which probably refers to the convention on asylum signed in that city. Soon after Gebre arrived in Rome, he met someone who described himself as a Dubliner, but Gebre didn't know what it meant... *Two weeks, four weeks later* (another little stammer) ... in an Ethiopian restaurant behind the station he met a friend whom he knew from back home in Addis. Soon afterwards, two of the friend's acquaintances arrived in the restaurant, both from Eritrea, *here it doesn't matter*, presumably meaning that here it's not so important which part of the Horn of Africa you come from, here we're all in the same boat, even the Somalis. The men were wearing smart white shirts and ties, grey pressed trousers, they looked like civil servants working in an office. Almost immediately they said they were Dubliners, though one of them had been visiting family in London for several months, he'd managed to get a job, he had a roof over his head... Then they found his fingerprints in the system, and he was returned to Italy. That's what a Dubliner is... the ones who get sent back, said Gebre. He needed somewhere to stay, and the men told him they lived nearby and could sort him out with a place for the night. He took his bike (he'd managed to get himself a bike almost straight away, *just like in Addis*, he explained). They left the restaurant and walked off, he pushing his bike, to an area of Victorian palaces, villas, and greenery behind the railway station ... (I knew this area from my previous visits to Rome, embassies, diplomatic residences, tall walls running along the sides of the streets, decorative pine trees growing in the gardens; the area reminds me of Eira in downtown Helsinki, where Jori Henrik used to live, though here the impression is, if possible, even more affluent). The men stopped by one of the buildings. A row of trash cans lined the wall, but in other respects the building didn't stand out from the other buildings on the street, a late 19th-century three-story villa whose ochre walls, white pilasters and wrought-iron balconies on the upper floor gave an instantly favorable impression. *We stopped,*

a hand gesture to show that he wasn't expecting anything, *we just stopped*. While they were waiting in the
street, someone arrived from the opposite direction,
one of the house's inhabitants, he too possibly from
Eritrea. The new arrival greeted them and walked in
through the gate. Parked in the small yard behind the
gate were two Mercedes from the 1980s that looked
like they hadn't been driven for years. Their tires
were empty, and with the exception of their chassis,
the cars were nothing but scrap metal. The group
walked inside, and Gebre saw a row of mattresses
on the floor, men lying here and there. The building
used to be the Somalian embassy, though the water,
plumbing, and electricity had all been cut off twenty
years ago when the government in Mogadishu collapsed in 1991. The building had no central heating,
the toilets didn't work, and food was heated in tin
cans, in the most basic fashion, burning alcohol in
a vessel underneath… All 150 to 200 inhabitants relieved themselves into plastic bags, which they then
threw onto the street or dumped in the trash cans
outside. Every room, even the garage, was lined with
mattresses, one tight against the other. Clothes hung
above each mattress, and on the shelf behind the
clothes was a small carpet bag or suitcase containing
the men's scant belongings. In late summer, the air in
the rooms was like warm urine, someone said. In the
winter, the temperature could drop below freezing.

At night, there were fights over blankets or sleeping places. Gebre saw people sitting in the leather armchairs in the ambassador's former office and the Voltaire chairs in the dining room. All of the building's inhabitants were Dubliners, he said, *tutti dubliners.* He heard stories about men who for years had had no address except yahoo.com. He was most shocked by the sight of two men who seemed so engrossed in their game of chess that they neither saw nor heard anything going on around them. Gebre ran out of the building and into the yard, where a man sitting on a metallic spiral staircase greeted him and explained that he had tried to burn off his own fingerprints, but in five to ten days they always grew back to normal. *If you register here, you will be a Dubliner for the rest of your life*, the man told him. Gebre spent the night at the *Somali house* without sleeping a wink and left the following morning, resolving never to return, and despite what he had previously planned he decided not to register himself. *I didn't want to be a Dubliner for the rest of my life*, he said. (In Stockholm some time later, I came across a small news item explaining that the police had eventually emptied the former Somalian embassy in Rome. One of the residents, a young Somali man, had met an eighteen-year-old girl at the railway station and proceeded to rape her that same evening. The news item claimed that 140 inhabitants had been cleared from the building and driven out into the street. Some of them were ill or so weak that they could barely stand up.)

The hottest moment of the afternoon, the heat was taking its toll. Gebre was silent for a moment. We were lying on the grass, I'd crooked my arm under my head and closed my eyes when, there amid the sweltering heat, I heard in a soft voice, *in the morning ... 1 took my bicicletta and left, I decided I would never go back to the Somali house. I was lost ... and my mother, in Addis, she had died...* I was startled, but he added that this had all happened some time ago. His mother had been ill, but... He was trying to find the right word and didn't complete the sentence. For him, there would be no return home, the rest of his days would play out here... The bags of walnuts rustled nearby. All I could offer by way of response was to hand him a bottle of water that a city employee had given me as I'd walked out of the metro station. Gebre downed what was left of the water, his large Adam's apple bobbed up and down a few times, and after this he continued... *I was totally shaken...* He left the Somali house in the morning and wanted to go somewhere a bit more peaceful; the churches were full of tourists, but behind the Olympic stadium there are some wooded hills... He had once gone there, in someone's car. He rode his bike along the riverbank to the area around the stadium, the woodland lay behind it. One of the gates into the stadium was open, a group of workmen were standing further off, for a moment he walked his bike here and there before deciding to head right through the stadium to the woodland behind. Gebre chuckled, shook his head, stammered, *it was the wrong place, totally wrong...* I envisage him pushing his Pilen, his eyes lowered. Soon he told me that the road leading up to the stadium was covered from side to side with mosaics, and every few meters was the acronym DVCE DVCE, endlessly repeating like the cry of a vast crowd, he said. Next, he noticed in these images a group of large figures playing tennis, and in his flustered state of mind he even heard the players striking the ball with their racquets, moaning and panting as they played, and it was only a moment later that he realized the sounds were coming from a real tennis court that he couldn't see, somewhere behind the tall grandstand. He was horrified at the thought that there was nothing keeping him moored to the reality around him, and then... (again he stammered, it took a moment until he could gather himself and continue), then he saw three-engine aircraft in front of him, men in black suits, some kind of engineers with picks and shovels. A man in a black shirt was holding up a flagpole, and in front of him an Ethiopian saluted the Italian flag, his arm outstretched, next to the Ethiopian a lion bowed its head in resignation.

It felt wholly unreal; for a moment he played with the thought that this must be a delusion, though he knew it couldn't be. No, a delusion is when you cannot see what you're walking on, he said. People walk across these mosaics on their way to the stadium. The 1960 Olympics were held in that stadium, as was the final of the 1990 World Cup. All the big concerts take place there, Madonna and the like... Then I noticed that, a little further away, a workman had spotted me and was shouting something at me, I couldn't hear what and turned away... He was still agitated, or tense, instinctively shrugged his shoulders, tried to laugh... (In Stockholm, while I was going through materials related to Gebre's stories, I noted that the stadium had been renovated in preparation for the 1960s Olympics, as were the mosaics, the murals and inscriptions. The work was commissioned from the same company that had originally built the stadium at the behest of Mussolini's government. That's how history takes a step forward, practically and consistently, as if under the aegis of a collective night blindness.)

The mosaics, the shouting workmen... I jumped on my bike and cycled off, Gebre continued. Only once he got to the other side of the stadium, *into the woods*, as he put it, did he remember hearing that it was a place you shouldn't go alone, not even in the daytime... *I was upset, totally upset.* He held out his hands and gave a somewhat gauche shrug of the shoulders, then explained that he had to veer off the path to one side and crouch down behind a bush, *yes, for a shit*, he added... He could get himself killed and dumped in a gravel pit and nobody would ever find out where he was, he thought there behind the bush. As he squatted there pushing, tears welled in his eyes, he regretted not becoming a Dubliner back when he didn't even know what it meant. Now he didn't know what to do. Then, all of a sudden, right next to him, he heard the sound of crying, *yes, the cry of a baby ... and babbling — is it babbling in English...?* My grip on reality might have been disappearing, but at least I knew I was outside having a shit, not stuck in a maternity ward, he said (he stammered again, and again tried to lighten what he was telling us with a laugh). He soon realized that there were people nearby, and the crying was coming from somewhere further away behind the bushes... At the same time, and this felt like nothing short of a miracle, he said, I felt like I was present in the world, and I knew nothing except this world. If in the past I'd had an imagination, now it was gone. If in the past I'd imagined I could survive, though others had not survived, now I did not. Everything was here in this world, there was no beyond. If in the past I had lived in an imaginary world with hopes and fears, now I did not. I wasn't afraid of death any more than someone can be afraid of his own birth, he chuckled, and lying there on the grass he gave a wave of the hand as if to flick away the insects hovering in the air.

And finally, my two miracles... said Gebre a moment later, shaking his head as though he still couldn't believe what had happened. I was lying on my back on the grass, the boughs of the trees framed his face... His *two miracles. After* (hand gesture)... *I just wanted to live day by day, from bed to bed.* He laughed, said he knows all about Bodyform, Hästens, Jensen Royal. He met a Swedish girl, they lived together for two weeks (it soon turns out this is when he became Kurre), he had lots of relationships, Swedes, Norwegians, Germans, package holidaymakers and what have you. To the tourists, he learnt to be an Italian, from the south, Calabria or Puglia. Before long he knew everybody in Trastevere, every waiter, every hotel cleaner, even the hoteliers themselves. This was the life you live when you no longer expect anything. Then a *miracle* happened, he said (again he stammered, but now with a smile, this was gleeful stammering). It was morning, he was sitting in the piazza in Trastevere... a red-haired girl walked across the square carrying a plastic bag from a nearby grocery store. She was tiny (lying on the grass, he showed us how small she was, barely up to his shoulder). At that moment he didn't have anything in particular to do, so he stood up and watched where the girl was heading. He followed her up a narrow set of steps (I noted that this was the same route Mara and I had taken last Saturday). There is a little house up there, recently refurbished into a hotel, Gebre explained. The girl disappeared into the building. *A tourist, I thought.* Gebre walked round the corner of the building, behind it there was a small patio and a parking space. He heard the sound of a shower coming from an open window above him, followed by the slap of bare feet on the floor... *I was very excited, like never before*, he laughed. A few days later, this time in the afternoon, the girl walked across the square in the opposite direction. He set off after her, but the girl walked past the grocery store, ran off and disappeared into a tram... She didn't look like a tourist anymore. *I start to wait for her.* On the third or fourth day, the girl appeared again, and by now she felt so familiar that he said hello to her. *The next day she is my girlfriend... So, I meet a girl, and I fall in love, in due time* (again, gleeful, playful, self-deprecating stammering). The girl was from Ireland, she worked in a hotel, felt more at home in Rome than she did in Ireland, came from a poor family. *I slept with Ketty, no Hästens...* She didn't care that he was an illegal... The hotel was owned by a woman of around sixty, she accepted me, never asked any questions, said Gebre. On one occasion, when Gebre and his

girlfriend had had a few beers, she laughed and said
we should move to Dublin and that way one of us
will become a *real Dubliner ... pubs, walks along the
Liffey* (Gebre pronounced the name of Dublin's famous river like a real Irishman... and couldn't help
adding that at moments like these Ketty took to calling him *my Eamonn, my Edward...*). He spent the
night with the girl more often and started spending
more time at the hotel too, some afternoons the
couple would sit with the owner on the roof terrace.
I lived a normal life, he said, sometimes I did odd
jobs at the hotel... It was a miracle, and Ketty was...
Well, everything in his life felt sorted. He did his
little jobs, received a little wage, had his little girlfriend. Ketty's in Dublin at the moment, she's coming back in a few days, said Gebre, and she doesn't
know there is a law here, has been for some time...
a law that being in the country illegally is a crime...
just like renting an apartment to a... He left the sentence hanging, made another telling hand gesture.
He wasn't just a criminal, he was liable to receive
a sentence a third longer than others for the exact
same crime simply because he was an illegal... And
because he was an illegal he couldn't marry either,
or so he'd heard. If he were to father a child, would
he even have the right to acknowledge paternity?
This is my second miracle, now I'm a criminal, he said,
stammering through.

Dinner time was approaching, and we decided to eat at a nearby restaurant. The place advertised itself as a harborside taverna, though the coast was at least twenty kilometers away. Besides us, the spacious restaurant was empty. The interior design, the furniture, the plants, decorative fruit and so on, were all made from some kind of industrial plasticine, the whole place was a veritable fake farmhouse, which I must have thought because the criminal, whom I couldn't consider a criminal, was a suitable customer in such a place, or then the legal system that had made him a criminal resembled this phony taverna. Our table had been painted to represent a tree trunk cut off at the root, next to us stood a fake fig tree, tangles of leaves, crates of coal, a terracotta stall with all manner of hams and salamis and other sausages hanging from it, braids of garlic, bunches of red and white grapes, on the counter there were bowls of peaches, apples, and other fruits, all with green leaves as though they had been plucked from a local farmyard only a moment ago, chili peppers, small woven punnets, large bread baskets, corn cobs, lanterns, copper pans, awnings, an impressive meat counter, candles propped on a wine barrel had dripped trails of wax halfway down each side of the barrel, in the corner of the room was a ladder, presumably used to pick oranges. With the exception of the wooden ladder, everything was fashioned from the same industrial plasticine or concrete. We no longer spoke about Kurre's experiences in Rome, but his words betrayed a certain vulnerability when he told us that the *oldest* church in the Vatican is Ethiopian, that Christianity arrived in Ethiopia *at the same time* it arrived here, or that *all humans are from Ethiopia*, which he said as he took a scrap of bread and mopped up the remains of the sauce on his plate. He ordered one beer after another, which an anxious-looking Mara duly paid for.

As we leave the restaurant, Mara invites me to join them, and I wonder whether he is worried about Gebre. We walk toward the apartment, Gebre sees an all-night convenience store and pops in to buy two bottles of vodka. He says he likes *Kossu*, as he now calls Koskenkorva, he likes *clear spirits*, and they make excellent *clear spirits* in the Nordic countries, so he should visit for this reason alone. He suddenly mentions the department stores and subway stops of Stockholm, *Åhléns, T-bana, Sergel Square*. Kurre (for that is what he sounds like right now) starts talking about *spirits* and Sweden and says he'd like Mara to help him get there. When he drinks *Kossu* or other *spirits*, he imagines the north, the pristine forests, the *nightless night*. Kurre didn't like Mara's answer that it would be quite a journey to get to Sweden and there was always the possibility of complications because he didn't have a valid passport or any other documentation and his old passport had an Italian tourist visa with an entry stamp but no exit stamp. In a somewhat more intense tone of voice, Gebre switched Sweden for Switzerland, at least Mara could help him get there, Switzerland isn't even in the Schengen area. This led to a quarrel between them. Switzerland may not be a signatory to the Schengen Agreement, but it nonetheless upholds the principles of that agreement, said Mara, one would become a Dubliner there too, but Gebre argued the point, saying if he could get to Switzerland, he would be safe. He was angry, but as if to lighten the mood, he said he just wanted to travel, to see places, he wanted to go to Venice, to which Mara simply said it's awash with tourists. Gebre replied that he wants to visit Venice and he wants to go there with Ketty, he wants to get Ketty *pregnant* (hand gesture), *really pregnant*, he added (even bigger hand gesture). He *wants to father a child to live in freedom* (another kind of hand gesture), but Ketty was in Dublin, something had happened and she had to stay there, he explained when I asked when she was coming back, *two weeks, two months*, he shrugged his shoulders.

We arrive at a residential area with new, five-floor, gentrified apartment blocks. We walk across the forecourt to the nearest doorway, and a moment later we are sitting around a coffee table in a large studio flat. It belongs to one of Ketty's friends, says Gebre, no, the friend is from England, not Dublin.

Gebre takes a bottle of vodka from his satchel, carefully unscrews it, as though he is removing a fish from a hook to throw it back in the water, he fills the glasses and immediately downs his own, the *clear spirits* will carry him to freedom, to the fjords and pine forests of the north, to Skjolden and Yertsevo, I thought, though the latter could not be further removed from the notion of freedom. Gebre hadn't told us why he'd left Ethiopia, and with all the coincidences and contradictions of what he had told us in the park that afternoon, the precise circumstances of his departure remained unclear.

Despite Kurre's sympathetic demeanor, I felt a spontaneous suspicion toward his stories (I was slowly beginning to adopt the name that Mara used for him). Presumably he believed he had to adapt the stories about his life, fit them into a mold that we would find acceptable, or that he thought we would find acceptable. My attitude might have been cheap, realistic, or ridiculous, but it certainly wasn't unusual. The NKVD agents who interrogated Herling had thought the same. Now Kurre was counting timetables the way those in the gulag measured bread, to the last crumb, perhaps even his smile was akin to Herling's hunger strike, which he began after waiting four months to be released with the remaining

Polish prisoners in accordance with an agreement signed with the Russians. Only now did I notice that the bottle of Wódka Wyborowa was Polish too. Kurre told us he had entered Italy on a tourist visa, bribed a clerk at the consulate. Beyond that, he didn't elaborate on his arrival in Italy. At one point that evening he pondered how to build a life here, but he didn't have any particular thoughts on the matter. How could he? Vodka, *kippis*, he had learnt in Finnish, *cheers*. Everything he told us about his childhood involved being on the move. For as long as he could remember, they had moved from one place to another, and his mother had told him that the family had moved around like this when she was young too. Back then, people traveled here and there carrying grain, textiles, coffee, butter and raw cotton or fleeing places where fighting had broken out. On the outskirts of the capital, people rented mattresses and iron bedframes for a week or a month at a time. Fleeting memories... He and his mother sheltering from the rain under a tin roof... Seeing someone cycling past with his hands in his pockets... A boy of eleven falling in love with the bar lady, as they were called, at every long-distance pit stop (night falls, the grass is fragrant, the air is warm, the distant sound of voices, music, electric lamps under awnings, as I imagine with a glass of vodka in my hand). To the travelers and truck drivers these bar ladies sold beer and, to a select few, themselves. People were always eating pasta, everywhere, the Italians had brought pasta to the country, and prostitution and the fact that people travel from one place to the next, he said.

When Gebre was born, his mother's younger brother left Ethiopia and set off along the course of the Nile. At first I didn't understand what Kurre was trying to say about his uncle's departure, *camminare*, his long, balletic fingers strutted along the table top, his uncle had left Ethiopia *on foot*, bound for Sudan. *Camminare, walking, kippis.* While in Sudan, his uncle's shoes were stolen. Behind the table, Kurre raised his bare foot, propped it on his knee and tapped the sole of his foot with his fingers, *un mese, one month*. His uncle walked barefoot for a full month, through Sudan and southern Egypt all the way to Cairo where he remained for six months, *no papers...* One evening the Cairo police stopped him in the street (near Tahrir Square, from my own trip to Cairo I recalled the evening streets, the small neighborhoods, the military police stationed along the street twenty or thirty meters apart, the white uniforms, black epaulettes on their shoulders, black berets on their heads, they were elegant and they had an extremely bad reputation). The military police ordered his uncle to get into the back of a truck and drove him to Aswan. From there, another truck drove him to the southern border. The journey took more than a day, nine hundred kilometers, said Kurre. Upon arrival at the border, his uncle was shoved off the truck and the police ordered him to walk south, back across the border. His uncle waited ten minutes until the truck had disappeared, then started walking back again. A month later, he arrived in the same shared apartment in the suburb of Shubra where he had had a mattress on the living-room floor before his arrest. Another six months in Shubra, then his uncle made it to Canada. There he met an Italian woman, got married, and now he lives in Turin. *This was twenty years ago.*

Kurre is smiling, his eyes unable to focus, and it's hard to understand him, he is drinking, slurring his words and stammering. I understand only a smattering of Italian, his English is getting ropier. *Yes, and three million years ago…* if I understand what he's saying. *Awash, you know what is Awash…?* He laughs but doesn't wait for my response. He fills our glasses with vodka; the glasses on the table are all different, there weren't three alike in the cupboard. *This was three million years ago…* Humans come from Ethiopia, everyone comes from Ethiopia, this bit I understand. A moment later, Kurre returns to the subject, *Awash, you know.* Painfully slowly, I gather from his slurred speech that Awash is a river, a place, a remote region, and somewhere there is a *rift*, a *depression…* Kurre talks, Mara lies on the couch, interprets now and then... *Yes, in seventy-four... French, Americans...* Somewhere there were French and Americans... *In Awash, on the left bank... They found half of the bones... twenty-nine kilograms, one hundred and ten centimeters...* (Kurre's bleary eyes, his dazed expression, he leans closer) *and walked like you and me.* A group of researchers had found the remains of a female being who had lived three million years ago, the same animal as humans, Mara interpreted, the bones had been preserved in volcanic ash. *Almost like Ketty*, said Kurre, again indicating his shoulder height, *but her name was Lucy.* Only now did I realize Kurre was talking about *the* Lucy. *You know, Lucy... Lucy in the Sky with Diamonds*, he sang. At their camp, the French and American researchers celebrated the discovery through the night, everybody knows that, said Kurre, they drank and sang and danced, and *Lucy in the Sky with Diamonds* blared out from their tape player over and over. Sometime during the night, the discovery was named *Lucy*, and now people know her name all around the world. Kurre got a little emotional as he told us about this discovery, repeating at regular intervals that all people come from Ethiopia and, in fact, the entire human race is from Ethiopia, *you see*, that's where humans originated, they left and spread across the world, *everyone comes from Ethiopia.*

Kurre's talk of Lucy and rural Ethiopia gave him the sense that he was just like everybody else, his illegal status momentarily forgotten, he seemed to forget it himself, his eyes calmed, his muscles relaxed, his laughter was free, as though the vodka's forty-volt haze had clarified the sobering notion that no man is master of his own destiny, and though we are all responsible for our actions, everything we do, we do unaware... I burst into laughter, on the other side of the table Kurre is singing *Lucy in the Sky with Diamonds* at the top of his lungs... He stands up, walks into the kitchen, opens the fridge and starts making an omelet on the gas stove, he is *starving*, he says and taps his stomach, those tiny restaurant portions won't keep you going for long. Soon afterwards, he brings the omelet to the table and douses it in vodka. Nobody should live a life like this (Kurre is referring to himself, he shakes his head)... People should have a sense of proportion toward one another, he says.

I can't make out his Italian, let alone his English, but he is talkative, and I try to keep up, though it remains unclear what he is talking about, something about a Dubliner or an illegal. He is standing behind the table, his feet tight together, as though he were unable to move... But hey, someone once said that even if you have to live your whole life on a cliff or a ledge, somewhere so narrow you can barely move your feet, there's just enough room to stand on the spot, and there's nothing around you but an abyss or an ocean, darkness and loneliness, even if there isn't any more space than that, half a square meter for the rest of your life, well (hiccup, stammer), it's still better to be *there*... Kurre goes into the kitchen, drinks a glass of water, and I soon hear the familiar metallic click as he cracks open another bottle. He staggers as though he were on a boat, the thought probably came to me from his monologue invoking the crashing ocean, boats crossing the Mediterranean by night, there in the darkness taking on water with every passing wave... *A toast to life!* Kurre raises his vodka glass, soon he is explaining something about how *only two thousand people* had held their nerve and survived a volcanic winter some tens of thousands of years ago. (In Stockholm later on, Kurre's talk of cliffs and ledges made me think of Agge sitting on the mountainside above the Red Cross camp, and of Dostoyevsky, perhaps someone in the Somali house was reading Dostoyevsky too; they played chess there, after all.)

We are all tired and try to sleep. I remain on the couch; they go to the mattress on the other side of the room. I have just dozed off when I awake to a sound, half-asleep. At first I think a table must have toppled over, then I hear a sound like two wild boars rutting; across the room, Mara and Kurre are having sex. It sounds as though Kurre is throttling Mara to death.

I lie on the couch, unable to get back to sleep, and start going through the things we talked about during the course of the evening. I'd asked Kurre about his family in Ethiopia, but he was clearly reluctant to answer. He said nothing about his father, did he even know his identity, his father could have been an Italian. Was Kurre's mother one of those bar ladies selling beer, the kind that an eleven-year-old boy might fall in love with? It was as though I was trying to interpret an ashen archive, just as Björling had interpreted his own, only this ashen archive didn't merely contain Kurre's life but extended to other people and things too. Something was happening across the room. They were both laughing now, and the laughter continued as they had sex, and the more they had sex, the jollier it sounded.

At some point in the early hours, Kurre is lying on his back on the mattress, his chest raised, am I hearing right, he's whimpering, with joy, despair, something, then a moment later everything is perfectly still, and I assume they must have fallen asleep. Kurre grinds his teeth, talks in his sleep, tossing and turning on the mattress, and I guess he must be sweating too, like Mara said. I doze off for a moment, then wake up, thirsty, I stagger through the darkness into the kitchen, flick a switch that I think is for the small lamp above the sink, but it switches on the main light on the ceiling, Kurre stirs on the mattress, *switch off the lights*, he snaps.

I awoke shortly after five in the morning, once I sensed it was already light behind the curtains. I lay on the couch, the pines were fragrant, the sunny day just beginning, unless I was dreaming of the summer mornings of bygone years and the pine trees of east Helsinki. I got up and stepped into the kitchen, but as there was still some time before my departure and Kurre and Mara were still asleep, I went back to the couch, I think I even dozed off again because the light and the forests beyond the curtains turned into a world where life carries on one day at a time, as it had in the stories of *One Thousand and One Nights*, and each morning Mara raises first one hand, then the other, just as G.E. Moore had done before him. It was Mara who first told me about the British empiricists who said the contention that the sun will not rise tomorrow is no less intelligible (and implies no more contradiction) than the affirmation that it will rise. When I leave at noon, Kurre gets up, I watch as his long, proud, balletic fingers button up his Lindeberg shirt. *I'm glad I met you*, he says. That's what people say, I suppose.

Half an hour later, I look out over the southern panorama of the city as my taxi drives along an elevated motorway on its way to the airport. The giant dice at EUR stands taller than the trees. Kurre and Mara were somewhere behind it, Kurre in the shirt Mara had bought from Stockmann's, perhaps Mara had given him other clothes besides, a Noah's ark of garments, the kind of miscellany Björling had asked his brother to send. If Kurre's life is a mess, it's not his own fault, Mara said that morning. *Unlike my parents or relatives, he actually has some serious goals in life.* In the past, Mara's own parents had caused him so much grief that he wanted to know who this man was, this Ethiopian who at first had succeeded in causing so much grief of his own. Mara's relatives wouldn't have liked him, and they would have particularly disliked the idea of his giving clothes and a little money to someone like Kurre, he explained. The previous evening, Kurre had had his own understanding of who was on the winning side. Every year the wind carries a hundred million tons of *fertile* soil to Italy, *for free.* Here fruit and vegetables grow in *their soil, their mud and clay,* then the people follow it, they come here to pick tomatoes and fruit for a risible hourly or daily wage.

On the plane, I read Herling's book about the gulag and looked at two sepia photographs of the twenty-year-old author, one taken from the front and one in profile, with his details in Cyrillic lettering underneath. He looks determined in these photographs, yet almost like a child, and after this he was made a criminal, his life irredeemably transformed. Herling and Kurre were both the same age when they were turned into criminals, I thought. Last Saturday,

I was at Lante listening to a conversation about the thirty-kilometer barrier for marathon runners. Yesterday, Kurre had spoken as though he was constantly running. Just as Kurre no longer has a place in the world and is excluded from the ways of the world, thought no longer has a place in the world either, it too is excluded from the ways of the world, Mara said later that night. In the end, all thought is thrown out with the trash just when you need it most. The very fact that thought doesn't matter leads to Kurre and people like him being turned into criminals, said Mara. A week ago, everyone at Lante had introduced themselves as docents or stipendiaries, writing a PhD or researching such-and-such. *I am a cat buried alive*, Kurre said last night. We have all been spoilt by an easy life, and everybody just accepts it, *that's the way the cookie crumbles*, said Mara. We are accustomed to our easy lives, just as those at the camp had to become accustomed to a life that was anything but easy, then sever all ties with the past, as Herling writes. *It's nothing, you'll get used to it.* With these words, new arrivals at the camp were inducted into the conditions that awaited them, and before long their memories of normal everyday life felt overwhelming, painful. Sometimes, the unconscious imitation of their previous life helped them to cope with their new conditions, while forgetting all about it gave them the best prospects for the

time ahead. Those who have a simple faith survive
best of all. When a prisoner learns on his last day in
the camp that his sentence is to be extended indef-
initely, he returns to the barracks, he has suddenly
aged ten years, and by around four or five o'clock in
the afternoon, he is dead. Herling documents the
ways in which different people react to catastrophes.
A Polish priest offers absolution for two hundred
grams of bread, an old Uzbek reads the prisoners'
hands for three hundred grams. You can escape the
camp by committing suicide. Over the decades, and
until his death in 2000, Herling writes about char-
acters all struggling with the same dilemma: hope
or despair. Without hope, we cannot live, but at the
camp, anyone clinging to hope loses the final opportunity to impact his own life. Hope has us running
after all kinds of whims, it makes us sly compared
to those who have no hope at all. When the Pope
arrived in Naples in November 1990 and spoke at
the Piazza del Plebiscito, right next to Gambrinus,
Herling did not see hope around him, the *speranza*
that that occasion proclaimed. I read Herling and
thought about Kurre. Of course, the two cannot be
compared. Herling was in a gulag where only one in
every hundred survived. All Kurre can look forward
to is an endless limbo without any real prospect of
salvation. Still, I was taken aback when I found a situation in Herling's text that Kurre had recounted in

almost exactly the same words, the prisoners would sit around in a ring and pass a shared cigarette from one man to the next when there weren't enough to go around.

I didn't stay in Helsinki but drove through the night to Uukuniemi. In a single week, Finland had turned green, the embankments were brimming with cow parsley, wild lupins and, once I passed Lappeen-ranta, Russian lorries. From Imatra onward, Russian signs by the roadside advertised fresh pike, white-fish, smoked fish. When I got back, I was relieved to see that the birches had been chopped up and taken away. There were splinters and sawdust everywhere, as if from an explosion, the fence had collapsed and the chunks of the birch trunk, cut with a chainsaw, had been dumped on the neighbor's land along-side the remains of all the other birches that had come down in recent years, but there were enough trees still standing that these two birches certain-ly wouldn't be the last. This time yesterday Kurre was raising a glass of vodka in EUR, *a toast to life*, I thought as I noticed there were chanterelles on the hillside, a red clover pushed its way through the sand between some concrete blocks. It had been raining, hence the chanterelles and the mounds of sand that the ants had piled up. When it rained heavily, water gathered in puddles, blocking the entrances to the colony. Once the rain stopped, it only took a few hours for the ants to clear the sand away, and the entrances to the tunnels were operational again. In Kontula, I had tried in vain to get Mara interested in ants. *The combined weight of all the ants in the world is equal to the combined weight of all the humans in the world. Ants carry life itself because they care for their offspring.* Mara stood next to the anthill, using a branch with a few leaves at the end to bat away the mosquitoes, half-listening, but despite my best efforts, he never showed any interest in the subject.

In late July, the temperature at Uukuniemi rose to 30°C every day. In the morning, the horseflies would attack aggressively by the shore. I thought of Mara and Kurre, though the reason surely wasn't the *African weather*, as I heard someone say at the grocery store, as if to explain why two burly border guards had headed straight to the freezer compartment to pick out ice-cream cones. The following day the air was thick with heat and the acrid smell of smoke. The opposite shore was only one and half kilometers away, shrouded in a bluish haze. *Ivan's on his siesta*, I heard at the store every summer, meaning that on the Russian side of the border they didn't even try to put out forest fires until the flames started threatening the villages. When I returned to the cabin in the early afternoon, the temperature was 32°C, an hour later it was 33°C. On the news it said that Moscow was baking in thirty-seven-degree heat and that the city was suffering from smoke caused by forest and peat-bog fires. Several wasps found their way into the cabin in the early hours; on one occasion, I opened my eyes to find a wasp on the pillow next to me. The following night I leave the window open, it's unbearably hot indoors, sleep comes in fits and starts. I wake at half past four to the reek of smoke. That afternoon a temperature of 37.2°C had been measured at Joensuu airport. I'd spent the day sweating and reading whichever of Herling's books were to hand, one after the other.

The evening news warned of inclement weather. There was a front coming in overnight. People at the grocery store had been saying for days that *the weather has gone mad*… Ten minutes before midnight, the electric lamp starts to flicker (as though I was rapidly blinking my eyes). I decide to go outside and look at the sky. Because of the mosquitoes, I'm in the habit of quickly pushing the door shut behind me, but this time one slam of the door and the whole cabin goes dark. Even across the shore the lights have gone out, a power cut. I try to get some sleep, but there is an expectant, uncanny charge in the air. *He sweats so much that the sheets are soaked through, but he says the most important thing is that he's allowed to be a part of all this.* Before long a whooshing sound whips up outside, and a few seconds later the wind hits. I get up and go to the window, then I run outside, the thirty-meter pine trees are swaying back and forth in the wind, as if shaken by an *unknown hand.* The shorter pines, their trunks the width of a thigh at the root, appear to arch toward the ground. The wind continues for ten or fifteen minutes. After this comes a heavy downpour. The lightning continues for a few hours. By morning, the storm is further away, judging by the seconds between the flash and the boom of thunder, I counted to twenty. The following day, the power is still off, there is less than a canister of drinking water left, the carbon water filter isn't working, the fridge has thawed, but outside it feels almost cool, only 26° C. In a single night, nature had assumed its late-summer colors. The energy company explains that large areas are without electricity; an entire power line has disappeared. It will take weeks to repair the damage across the local area, with volunteers traveling along the power lines through the forests. The store fifteen kilometers away was closed, they had no drinking water either, and I heard that their freezers had thawed. At eight o'clock in the evening, the electricity buzzes into life, I warm some food and filter more drinking water, but at night the wind whips up again. Pinecones patter along the roof. The roof would fold like a sheet of paper if one of those tall pines came down on it. I've closed the windows, but the indoor temperature is becoming unbearable, and I have to open them again. Another storm hits us, not as powerful as the previous night, but enough to take out the power again. In the morning, I find in the shed an old portable gas stove that I haven't used for fifteen years. I drive to the store in Kesälahti to buy a gas cylinder for the stove. At the counter I hear that the E6 highway is closed off, as is the railway between Imatra and Parikkala; it will take a few days to clear the fallen trees from the tracks and repair the overhead contact lines. At a single campsite, fifty trailers have been damaged by falling trees. For the next three days I cook out in the yard with my stove. It's quiet, neither birdsong nor the buzz of insects, from the boughs of the tall trees a pinecone falls now and then and clonks on the concrete slabs. My phone is silent, the storm has done something to the cell towers.

From the moment I returned to Uukuniemi, I'd been trying to get on with my work on Herling, but even after the first few attempts, I knew it wouldn't continue. The piece wasn't a failure, everything I used to think about it was still true, but something else was awry. Initially, I thought I didn't really want to get to grips with my brother and, as it were, murder him, and concluded rather that his despair and digressions were his own, but this wasn't the whole truth, my own life resisted. His despair and digressions were a mirror image of my own. For years I'd been plagued by the feeling that I was drifting ever further away from people. The feeling kept recurring, and the occasional success did nothing to assuage it. My brother was living the very same life, and like other people, he too was trying to reshape the physical experience of the life that our father and grandfathers had lived. His rage, his jeering laughter, was a form of father-hunger. I'd perceived something similar in Kurre that night in EUR. When Wittgenstein renounced his inheritance, he wasn't only trying to struggle free of his past, as Mara's heroic retelling suggested, rather he was behaving as though his father hadn't died at all, as though there was no inheritance and everything was just as it had been before. When Atlantic salmon reach a certain age, they start swimming upstream through the rapids to spawn in the place where they were born, but for humans such a grand re-enactment of the life of the past doesn't work, even the strongest ties cannot hold, the world staggers onward, all that is solid melts into the air, and our daily paper bombs take care of the rest.

Everybody lives this impossible dream in their own, unique way, but reality does not reciprocate our dream of a sense of continuation, and as a result life changes, becomes dislodged and off-kilter, some-

thing happens, something akin to the aftermath of a
car crash or when someone is diagnosed with Alzhei-
mer's disease, they become someone else, they are no
longer understood as the person they once were, the
duck does not turn into a rabbit or vice versa, rather
the result is rabbits with quickly beating wings and
blue specula, and ducks with long ears, a coat of fur
and a bushy tail seven centimeters long. A heatwave
had settled over the region, and every day I went on
long walks, visiting places I had never been to in all
the years I'd been coming here. A few kilometers
away, a spruce forest had fallen in the wind, every last
tree. I walked for hours, plucked raspberries, gazed at
old, deserted farmsteads, their yards now overgrown.
The verandas of these abandoned houses were a clutter of disparate paraphernalia, one of the doors bore
a faded print where I could just make out the image
of an Alsatian and the text *Guard Dog on Duty*. The
border area was dotted with thicket-covered islets,
reed banks, small sandy shores, decades-old saunas,
in their sheer inaccessible remoteness they would
have been suitable places for me and my brother, I
imagined as I walked past them. I would tell him
about the Ethiopian, the day and night in EUR,
Kurre's hopes and aspirations, *pubs, walks, Awash, a
toast to life, cheers* and so on. I don't know what my
brother would tell me, his life must have had its own
mishaps, its agonies and miracles, maybe his aspira-

tions were the same as the Ethiopian's, *pubs, cheers* and so on. My brother would step off the train at the station in Kesälahti, out of habit his fist would gently press against my chest. If he were here, we would walk out to the shore at the campsite, we would eat fish together, buy some beers from the store and heat up the sauna, but in this imagined scenario the electricity had been reconnected, the fridge was working and the world was different. Should I tell him that for Herling any catastrophe was a brutal, blind event, that in the gulag life even began to drain from the living, thoughts and feelings disintegrating until all that was left was a life burnt bare? My Herling piece was the last in a long string of corrective measures by which I retroactively tried to alter the events of my childhood, my family history; to my brother I was faithful the longest, just as faithful as he was to me when he once drunkenly fell asleep in the crook of my arm. My Herling piece was over because something had happened to the hopes associated with it, they were gone now, they had become unreal, as though the pines that had swayed so forcefully in the wind were suddenly floating in the sweltering air.

As I waited for the electricity to come back on, I had time to watch the bustling of the ants. Natural scientists tell us that, in order to understand ants, you have to watch more than one ant at a time. Ants react to one another. An individual ant encounters other ants, and only then decides what it is going to do next. According to scientists, what is decisive is not what that individual ant, as it were, tells the other ants during this encounter, but quite simply the fact of the encounter itself. *If the life of ants contained meanings the way human life does, for ants meaning would manifest when their paths cross*, I thought. The Finnish myrmecologist Rainer Rosengren studied ant colonies in Siuntio and Espoo's Westend in the 1970s, and he noticed that over a period of decades an individual ant colony can remember the route from their anthill to a particular tree where the ants can milk aphids for honeydew. In the springtime, the ants that have survived the winter guide the newly born ants along the route taken by previous generations. This way, a memory emerges within the colony. Memory and paths are linked for ants just as memory and paths are linked for humans. At around midnight, I take a torch and walk down to the jetty, there are no lights along the opposite shore, no signs of life. Aspen saplings a few meters tall stand next to the cabin, and in the torchlight I can see ants scuttling in two directions along their slender trunks, even in the dark the ants were navigating to their aphids. But nobody knows what makes ants turn simple encounters on their paths into decisions about what to do next or about how to work without advance planning, how to dig a tunnel and where to pile the bodies.

As the weekend approached and phone service was up and running again, Mara called early one morning and said that Kurre had disappeared. He had left the apartment in EUR, and Mara hadn't been able to reach him for several days. Late the previous evening, Kurre had called from Turin, he was at his uncle's place, but something was wrong. *No, he wasn't coming back to Rome*, Kurre had refused to discuss the matter, and eventually Mara had suggested he travel to Turin so they could meet. First thing that morning, Mara had hunted down the uncle's contact details and called him. The uncle answered, but he was unwelcoming. *I have own life, twenty years already... Yes, gone, Switzerland*, that's the impression he had of Gebre's whereabouts. It might have been true, said Mara. While in Rome, Kurre had talked about Switzerland, imagined he'd be able to organize things better there. They'd had an argument about this only a few days ago. Earlier that evening, Kurre had got himself picked up for shoplifting a bottle of water, and when he couldn't produce any paperwork, the store's security guard knew what was going on. Mara had paid the guard two hundred so he wouldn't call the police. *Two hundred*, said Mara. That's what it's like being *vogelfrei*, Ludde's word, by which he doesn't mean free as a bird but being an outsider, an outlaw, a sitting duck that anybody could shoot. Kurre could have asked me to buy him a bottle of water, said Mara, it was a completely pointless row. Eventually, Kurre had flown into such a blind fury that he had *slapped* him, as Mara put it. After that, they hadn't seen each other. I imagined Kurre tense, agitated and withdrawn, his knee twitching next to the table leg as it had in the restaurant in EUR when he'd told us about his situation. Mara had decided to go to Turin, the *freccia* would be leaving in two hours and would pull into Porta Nuova in Turin at two thirty in the afternoon. He would ring Kurre once he arrived. I told Mara it sounded like he was looking for trouble, or something worse still, and that Kurre was abusing him, shamelessly. What do you expect, Mara replied. Kurre needs help finding every meal, every bottle of water, so of course he abuses people, that's what everybody does, *even those who don't need to*. I told Mara that I thought he saw the catastrophic aspects of his own life reflected in Kurre, and that's why he felt such a strong desire to help him. Ultimately, we set out to help ourselves though we tell ourselves we want to help others, I said several times. On my part, this was a genuine expression of concern, one that aroused a fear that one morning Mara would wake up to find himself lying in a gravel pit, robbed or worse. Mara was full of ice-cold rage and reiterated that Kurre's life is a mess, and he isn't responsible for that himself.

By the afternoon, Mara was in Turin, where he called me multiple times, sometimes barely a few minutes apart. He was trying to call Kurre, walking through the city center, he visited an Ethiopian restaurant near the railway station but didn't stay to eat. On the station concourse, a flock of pigeons fluttered into flight to avoid the bustle and the announcements and settled in the steel frames in front of an art deco window standing the height of the wall, and when Mara finally got hold of him, they could barely talk on the phone for all the clamor, I heard right away. Kurre was in Aosta, about twenty kilometers from the Swiss border. Mara had asked him to stay put where he was, in a café somewhere in the center of Aosta, and he would meet him there. Kurre had replied that he didn't intend to come back to Rome and asked Mara to help get him across the border and into Switzerland. Outside, across the square in front of the station, a silver-grey bus was about to leave for the two-hour drive to Aosta. Ten scheduled departures a day, every hour, covering the hundred-plus-kilometer journey, but Mara saw a Hertz office and decided to rent a car instead. At least I can enjoy the scenery, he chuckled. Kurre had taken the same route to Aosta yesterday or that same morning, he's trying to get a car to take him to the border, not through the tunnel but along the Great St. Bernard Pass, tourists drive up and down that route until September.

Kurre would get out of the car by the roadside shortly before the border, Mara assumed. *I mean, who's going to take a complete stranger across the border...?* I too was familiar with the scenery along the St. Bernard Pass from a couple of years back, though traveling in the opposite direction, from Switzerland to Italy, as I told Mara before we ended our call... At the highest point along the route, surrounded by dark, craggy, snow-covered mountain tops, there was a plateau, cars parked along the road, their doors open, tourists standing by their cars taking in the views. *Wie eine Mondlandschaft*, bright as the lunar landscape... On the other side of the road is a small clear lake, with the border running down the middle of it. Standing on the Swiss shore is a white building five or six floors tall, the old hospice. Seen from the border and looking back toward Aosta, the terrain looks like the Arctic coast of Lapland, rocks, lichen, moss, flowers that thrive in the north, glacier buttercups, mountain avens, purple saxifrage, and the Alpine cousins of the forget-me-nots growing along the streams of England. Further down the mountainside, fog and rainclouds drifted low, barely half a meter from the ground... The road down to Aosta wound like a serpent every few hundred meters, and there seemed to be no end to the descent, ten minutes, half an hour, down and down, the path lined with gravel, rocks, and shrubs, further down there were valleys, meadows, small coniferous forests, Alpine buildings with slanting rooves... Kurre would laugh (I remember his laugh well, I heard it many times that night in EUR, an amused, almost deliberately child-ish laugh, followed straight away by another), *for him everything is an uphill struggle, for us it's downhill, the steeper his uphill, the gentler our downhill, the more he has to exert himself going uphill, the easier our life is...* We have lost sight of Kurre, I told Mara the next time he called, this time sitting in his Hertz rental car. I would never see Kurre again, and neither would Mara. You won't even find information about him online, I said. Yet the idea of Kurre wandering around the mountainous terrain of the St. Bernhard Pass wouldn't leave me in peace... That Ethiopi-an running step, 2,000 m above sea level... After the day's exertions, he might sit down somewhere, on a rock or a tree trunk, take off his shoes, rub his soles, inspect his feet... In the park he'd been wear-ing a pair of grey-blue Timberland running shoes, but in those conditions even Gore-Tex won't be much use, I remember the tongue bore the words *outdoor performance.* As morning breaks, Kurre is as deter-mined as Mara when he raised his hand into the air like G.E. Moore... Or perhaps he is sleeping in the pine and spruce forests further down the mountain-side, dreaming of a distant Dublin that he can bring to life with a kiss.

That evening, I waited in vain for Mara to call. I wandered among the bushes, picking gooseberries and blackcurrants, waiting for an update on Kurre. Smoke lingered in the air, *Ivan's siesta*, insects swarmed above the bushes, and the evening seemed overexposed, curiously beautiful. I tried calling Mara twice, but he didn't answer. I wanted to be in Aosta helping him to find Kurre. Mara was in Aosta, and Kurre was very likely there too, I thought. After a while, I remembered that Herling had written a story about Aosta too, and I started reading it to while away the time. Procrastination, I know, but the serene evening, the setting sun and the smoke from the forest fires across the border suited both the occasion and Herling's story.

Though I was reading to pass the time, and perhaps out of nervousness at what was happening in Aosta right now, from the very first lines of Herling's account it was as though he was in fact telling me about Kurre and about Mara looking for him, but Kurre was the protagonist, and almost immediately the story provided a path or link to Kurre and the evening's events. Everything that during the course of the evening or earlier that day had been left in the realms of speculation was answered in Herling's story. An unknown person became real, his struggles and desperation came to life, as though Herling himself had helped put me within sight of the person

Mara was trying to locate, and as I read on and fitted them both into the story and its milieu, I waited for a call from Aosta.

In the spring of 1944, after Herling had arrived in the Bay of Naples with Anders' Army, he fought along the Italian front until the end of the war against the Germans and their Italian allies, the latter under the command of Rodolfo Graziani, the bomber of Agge and Hylander's camps. The following summer, when fighting had ceased and Herling was transferred from a location near Bologna to Milan, he was granted a few weeks' leave. This was the first opportunity he'd had to rest since the outbreak of the war and his time in the gulag. In Milan, an Italian comrade gave him the keys to an empty house at Aosta, in the foothills of the Alps. At least, this is what Herling said in the story he published fifteen years later in 1960. The story is called 'The Tower,' and the title refers to a real tower in Aosta, still standing to this day, which the narrator only learns about when, in his friend's house, he happens upon a book by Xavier de Maistre entitled *The Leper of Aosta*, printed in Naples in 1828. Herling (or the narrator of the story, but to my mind that particular evening Herling *was* the narrator, because such was the life he had lived that he came to see and recognize all the things around him that the narrator describes), indeed, Herling begins reading Maistre's book, whose subject most probably reminded him of his own experiences.

When Herling later begins writing his own account, Maistre and the leper illustrate for him what a catastrophe really is. With their help, he is able to fully perceive what happened to him, he later wrote when he recalled this story on the nights following the Naples earthquake. Whereas pestilence is a catastrophe that severs the bonds between people, leprosy strikes one person at a time, forcing him into eternal solitude, for it is a disease that does not kill, but from which one can never recover. As with Herling's story, Maistre's story features a narrator strongly resembling the author himself, a man who arrives in Aosta, where he subsequently spends some time. Almost by accident, Maistre becomes fascinated with the tower and its garden and, as Herling recalls, when Maistre met the leper confined in the tower, his curiosity instantly turned to sympathy, he even wanted to shake the man's hand, though the leper kindly asked him to refrain from doing so.

Herling speculated that the very consolation of Maistre's book may well have interested the lonely teacher, who had recently lived in the same house, but it soon transpires that the teacher had in fact started to gather even more information on the leper in the tower. In Herling's eyes, the teacher's life of hermetic silence resembled that of the leper, and one of the few things known about the teacher was that he had lost his entire family in the Messina earthquake of 1908. When Herling eventually depicts the episode leading to the teacher's death, he draws a comparison to Maistre's leper as, in their own ways, both responded to a sympathetic guest by saying that all hope is gone. A provincial priest visited the teacher, but at the end of the war, when the Germans shoot the priest and the teacher witnesses what happened, the teacher returns to his house and dies that same evening. Herling explains that the house where the teacher lived was known locally as *the coffin*, Herling refers to the leper's tower as *the house of the dead*, a term he had earlier used in reference to the camp at Yertsevo.

Almost with a sense of horror, I wondered at the way everything repeats, at how the lines of Herling's story opened up a panorama in which locations, people, and situations were all intertwined. Maistre's 19th-century story resembles another series of events, one that Herling only learnt about in the summer of 1945, and both resemble the situation playing out now, sixty-five years later. In all three instances, events recur in such similar fashion that I have to draw breath and go outside to stretch my legs beside the gooseberry bushes. The smell of smoke had disappeared from the air, but the horror that I still felt reminded me of Rosengren's ants whose collective memory survived from one year, one decade to the next, keeping alive the paths along which the ants travel to their aphids.

Evening was turning to night, it was already past eleven o'clock, Mara should have reached the Swiss border long ago. I'd asked him to call me as soon as he had any news. He had probably already gone back to Aosta and was preparing to sleep in the cheap hotel he'd mentioned.

During the night, Herling's account (which also contains Maistre's account) transformed in my mind into a depiction of Kurre's life. From his tower, the leper gazes out at the mountaintops of St. Bernard. He gazes at the horizon as though it represents the future. Perhaps right now Kurre was gazing at the same mountaintops that the leper so dreamt about. Perhaps his heart too yearned to believe that beyond those mountains lies an unknown land where he can taste all the happiness he had dreamt of at night... When the first spring breezes blow through the valley, Maistre recalls, the will to live surges over the tower's inhabitant, sweeping away all obstacles in its path... The leper manages to flee his tower and becomes intoxicated on the vast open space around him. He wanders across the surrounding fields... He avoids other people, though he so keenly longs to meet them. He hides in the bushes on top of a hill like a wild animal, embracing the whole town with his gaze… He opens his arms to the residents and cries out with sheer unbridled joy… He hugs the tree trunks and prays, implores God to bring them to life and give him but one friend… On a forest path, he watches a pair of lovers who stop every few meters to embrace and kiss, and it's easy to imagine Kurre on that same path, probably thinking about Ketty.

I finish reading Herling's story at four thirty in the morning and wonder whether any of the three of us had slept at all that night. Mara was in Aosta, Kurre was wherever he was. The ability of the story to attest to Kurre's life lies in the fact that Herling and Maistre are able to create the experience of how a real person, who is flesh and blood, can attest to another person whose life was now nothing but the faint glow of ash. The leper in Maistre's story was a real person too, though little is known about him. Nobody knows exactly how old he was when he was taken to the tower, Maistre explains, but he must have been around twenty, just like Kurre. Maistre met the leper in 1797 and published the story about him fourteen years later in 1811. After the summer of 1945, Herling often visited Aosta. He recalls that on several occasions he tried to write about the leper's final years, that is, the years after he encountered Maistre, but each time he was struck by a sense of helplessness and had to put down his pen. He couldn't bring himself to imagine such *eternal solitude*. The very thought horrified him, just as it had horrified Maistre too. Herling published his own story in 1960. It contains only a few short snippets about the leper's final years. Herling describes his visit to the tower, which at first he couldn't find though it is right in the center of the town. Maistre tells us that the leper didn't know his own name and that he was very young when leprosy struck the family; Herling not only visits the tower but also names the leper as one Pier Bernardo Guasco, and he even learnt that Guasco (or Guascoz, as the name is spelt in some sources) survived for another six years after Maistre's visit. However, Herling was unable to establish the specific circumstances in which the tower's inhabitant eventually died. According to one version of the story, the leper hastened his own death through malnourishment. In another version, he was seen wandering the streets carrying a lantern, but the villagers' rocks and curses drove him back into the tower, where he soon perished. Herling says that this version must be related to another legend in which the door to the tower is haunted by a woman dressed in white and carrying a lantern. An online search quickly brings up images of the tower. In one picture, a few immigrants are standing in front of the tower, from Morocco perhaps, or the Balkans, red and white tracksuits, cheap garden sandals, one of them is sitting, the others standing around, it looks as though they have gathered there to kill time.

It's easy to imagine Kurre among them, had he happened to be there at the moment the photograph
was taken, but when Mara finally called me the following morning, he told me he'd been unable to find
any trace of Kurre, neither in Aosta itself nor at the
border.

The following day Mara drove back to Turin, called
Kurre's uncle and suggested they meet, I soon heard.
The uncle declined the invitation, citing either by way
of a reason or an excuse that he had spoken to Kurre
on the phone only the day before, and he had said
he was planning to call Mara. Mara asked whether
Kurre had called from Italy or Switzerland, but the
uncle answered curtly that he didn't know, and this
led Mara to believe that Kurre must still be on the
Italian side of the border. Ultimately, I don't know
anything about Kurre, but it's obvious he's trying to
get into Switzerland, said Mara before hanging up.
I envisaged Kurre amid the mountainous terrain
somewhere near St. Bernard... *Lucy in the Sky with
Diamonds* kept playing in my mind... Tourists in
their SUVs, bicycles secured to the back of the car,
motorcyclists at the serpentine bends in the road, in
August the tourist route is still heaving with traffic.
At one of the bends, Kurre jumps out of a car, thanks
the driver for the lift, continues on foot... Struggling
his way up the hills and inclines or hiking through

one of the small coniferous forests... sweat streaming down his head, his forehead, his back, though the air is chilly at 2,000m, *Lucy in the Sky with Diamonds* gives him renewed strength with every step... Mara said he didn't think Kurre would make it across the Alps. It'll be a miracle if he makes it as far as the border, and even then, he can't hang around there, he'll have to come back. In northern Italy an illegal can't get anywhere. Though on the surface you can't necessarily tell where Kurre is from, he'll end up in the hands of a gang of drunken vigilantes, said Mara, and for a moment I was plagued by the question of whether Kurre might still be wearing the shirt that Mara had once bought from Stockmann's.

At the library in Niukkala, I told Mailis about all this. She was curious, but even she concluded that this was the last we would hear of the Ethiopian. I was due to leave for Helsinki in a few days' time, but I promised to let her know if I heard any news.

I was packing my belongings when Mara suddenly called and told me he had received a call from Kurre. He was with someone or other in Biella, a small town about a hundred kilometers from Aosta, halfway to Milan. Mara couldn't establish who this unknown friend was, and even I wondered quite how Kurre had managed to find a roof over his head. People are empathetic to others when they believe their situations to be analogous, but nobody is empathetic to the illegals, not even other illegals, if Herling's writings on catastrophe are anything to go by, I thought as I continued packing. At the camp, everybody went to sleep terrified that this would be the night they met their end. Everybody felt a sense of helplessness because sleeping on both sides of them were men who were every bit as vulnerable to death as they were. Your neighbor's anxious whimpering reminded you of your own fate, and this was why it didn't elicit empathy. Shortly after Daniel Defoe published *Robinson Crusoe*, he depicted London during the plague, people giving one another a wide berth for fear of infection. The inmates at the camp behaved like this too. In the barracks, the fear of death drew everyone into a silent, selfish conspiracy, and everyone accepted this state of affairs, though they all knew that when their time came, they would be the next victim. Everyone remembered moments when they had lain on the spot, motionless, watching through barely opened eyelids as a body was carried out of the barracks, and everyone knew that their own appeals for help wouldn't stir the others from their begrudging apathy. But whereas Herling writes that, in everyday life, helplessness unites people in the face of death and calls for help do indeed elicit empathy, Kurre might well take a different view.

But at least Herling started writing, about the barracks and the leper of Aosta, and Wittgenstein climbed up into his observation post and discovered something ineluctable. Or did Maistre want to shake the leper's hand and Ludde climb up into his tower simply in order to end their own lives? That night, lying in bed before leaving for Helsinki, half-asleep or perhaps fully so, an endless stream of people climb up into towers and come down from them again, climb the Alps or up into their own observation posts, just like Agge on his ledge high on the mountainside, and most diligent of all are the ants scuttling up and down their aspen saplings, even at night, as I had witnessed by torchlight only a few days earlier.

Mara and his brain are always stumbling into things nobody else would stumble into, he never asked whether there was any sense in the formulation of a particular question, but he usually managed to hit on something important, no wonder he stumbled upon someone like that, said Hainari when I was in Helsinki and told him about Mara and the Ethiopian. The waves gently lapped a few meters away, the seagulls squawked, boats glided along the strait in front of Uunisaari, we were sitting outside a shoreside café in Kaivopuisto and had just ordered our first pints of Guinness. That's what the world has become, nobody looks ahead, said Hainari as he wiped a streak of Guinness froth from the corner of his mouth, fifteen years ago Jori Henrik at least caused some pushback with his talk of the end of the world, nowadays talk like that doesn't even have entertainment value. At most, people would say he has nothing original to say on the subject, just something elitist to say. And that the notion of the world's destruction is only topical because it hasn't happened yet. But Mara took it very hard when Red-Cheek passed away (these were Hainari's exact words), after that there was nobody to whom he even theoretically owed an explanation, Mara had said, referring to his decision to quit philosophy. Mara was sensitive about everything relating to Jori Henrik because, not only did he like him as a person, but it meant he was only a handshake away from Wittgenstein. A few months into his studies, Jori Henrik had asked Mara to compile an index for one of his books, as Hainari recounted at least once a year, and when Mara finally took the index to Jori Henrik's home on Laivurinkatu, out of the blue Jori Henrik suggested they dispense with the airs and graces and continue on first-name terms. A moment later, an elated Mara walked outside, glanced at the garden where there was a parasol, a table, chairs and a collie, he beamed at the dog too, it might have been Jori Henrik's own dog, and at that the dog got to its feet and started walking, limping on its hind leg.

When Mara turned and walked off toward the gate and saw the dog out of the corner of his eye, it was walking perfectly normally. When he stopped and turned to look at it directly, it started limping again. They repeated this charade several times. When the dog thought Mara was looking at it, it limped, but when Mara pretended to turn away, it walked normally. A dog cannot lie… Is it because he is too honest, Wittgenstein writes, and though these sentences don't actually have anything to do with dogs and their behavior, now there was a dog right in front of him, perhaps the philosopher's very own dog, play-acting, that is, lying, and thereby *slaying* Wittgenstein's claims. *The bill came right away*, Mara had said… People might think such things are stunning, though they are utterly ridiculous, but when Mara stumbles into an Ethiopian like this, you'd think there would be something insurmountable between them, said Hainari and ordered another Guinness. I hadn't told Hainari that Kurre had lied to Mara when the two first met, but I was reminded of this when Hainari recounted his habitual dog anecdote: Kurre had lied, but is it because he is dishonest? Still, Hainari saw some sort of family resemblance between Mara and the Ethiopian, as he proceeded to explain. Ultimately, Mara and the Ethiopian are the kind of brothers that curiously complement each other, I mean, their lives, he continued. I suppose he meant that Mara had lived through an era after which all that was left in the world was bread and circuses, and that the repercussions of that could be seen first and foremost in the impasse of a random Ethiopian. All thought is driven out of sight, and before long unpleasant things start to happen right in front of us, said Hainari, first of all to people with whom we don't have any obvious connection. In fact, the two of them, Mara and the Ethiopian, don't even complement each other, I mean, their lives, rather they belong together. This world turns someone like Mara or von Wright into an elitist clown and the Ethiopian into a survival clown. For the elitist clown, all thought is driven out of sight, and for the survival clown, all Ethiopians and those like him are driven out of sight, and if thought is not driven out of sight neither are the Ethiopians, said Hainari. Ultimately, the elitist clown and the survival clown are the kind of brothers that it's impossible to think about independently of each other, he said.

Hainari and I walked from Kaivopuisto toward the South Harbor. At the corner of Björling's house, I glanced up at the old maple with the tripartite trunk that had survived the bombing of February 1944 completely unscathed, though the building standing next to it had been razed to the ground, *life, a squirrel leap*. Björling coped, somehow, though he too was both an elitist clown and a survival clown, the former in his poetry, the latter because in the course of his life he hadn't even the paltriest income, even on his deathbed he still agonized over his enormous debts. Hainari and I parted company at the door of the Old Market Hall, and I spent some time wandering up and down the hall looking at the salmon counters. *Så godt for hjernen.* On several occasions, Mara had mentioned that the uncle in Turin was fed up with all the phone calls, and he asked whether I might call the uncle instead, I had met Kurre, after all. Heartened by my meeting with Hainari, I rang Turin, the uncle didn't sound very keen to talk, not exactly reluctant and not silent either. He said he'd heard that Kurre was dead. He said it so breezily that I couldn't believe it; yes, he'd heard it from another Ethiopian, a heart attack, that was his understanding of the matter, the uncle explained, still as though he were talking about the weather. Bewildered, I offered my condolences and promised to relay the news to Mara at a suitable moment.

After the phone call, I didn't know what to do. *It should have been my turn,* I recall from Mara's account of the funeral, *this is exactly how my name* or what was it. Kurre would hardly have claimed to have had a wonderful life, and for him, tomorrow mornings had always been in short supply. Later that evening, there was a program on television about the volcanic eruption in Iceland back in April, the reason I'd been unable to visit Mara earlier in the spring. A weary-looking woman in a woolen sweater recalled drinking her morning coffee by the window, she glanced outside and saw a wall of grey slurry running across the low-lying terrain... In a single night, the world turned black, the landscape was black, the sheep were black, the dog's kennel and the children's swings were black, the sky was an ashen grey, but otherwise the world was completely black... There was disbelief on the woman's face. The whole region was unrecognizable... In one week, the couple shoveled four hundred tons of ash from around their house... It was every bit as unfathomable as Kurre's life, that too blackened in one fell swoop when he was made a criminal.

The next day was a Saturday, in the afternoon I was due to meet my brother and our other family members. In the last ten years, I had only been to a handful of such occasions, and now I was meeting my relatives for the second time in a year, I thought as the boat crossed the narrow strait to the jetty outside the private restaurant at Uunisaari. When I arrived in Helsinki, I'd wondered whether I would be able to meet my relatives without thinking about the leper of Aosta, that is, Kurre, and now my mind was filled with news of his death. Even from the jetty, I could see through the tall panoramic windows twenty meters away, around fifty people in the dining hall, the same relative who had disowned me earlier in the spring sitting at the end of one of the long tables. Inside the dining hall it was noisy and bright, I sat down in the furthest corner by the window. Through the windows I saw the hundred-year-old black alders, the sandy shore, the islands with their sailing clubs, their boats and jetties, sunlight glinted on the water, and yet this grand, mute panorama was like a world apart, a place where different laws and rules apply. Whenever I visited the buffet table in the middle of the dining room (salmon, sesame-seeded, gingered, smoked and what have you), the voices and cadences around me and even the aggressive silence all reminded me of Kurre, and from a few snatches of conversation that were obviously intended for my ears, I learnt that my brother was already looking forward to something that would later come to be known as *the landslide*. [28] That afternoon, news of Kurre's death had struck me like a cold, personal *preliminary landslide*.

The meal was nearly over, and people were changing places, flitting from one chair to another, when I saw that my brother and a few other like-minded relatives sitting at the end of the table. One of my

28 The term *jytky* (here, 'landslide') refers to the electoral success-es of the nationalist, populist True Finns party during the early 2010s, which eventually led to their becoming one of the largest parties in the Finnish parliament.

older relatives recalled my early childhood, saying *he's been doodling from the moment he could hold a pencil*, and my brother and the others latched on to this right away. *He's had a doodling fixation from the time he was a kid.* A loud volley of laughter. *You can doodle all kinds of things.* I assumed this confected *doodling fixation* again referred to my supposedly mistaken ideas about the world, to *doodle* was to turn one's back on reality, whereas their *landslide fixation* was in touch with reality, it reflected facts, though in fact their fixation was mostly with *cartoons*, I thought to myself.

Looking at these people, one wonders what kind of landslides everyday life contained, even the kind of hateful landslides that pass from one generation to the next, landslides like flies, one on top of the other, flies that not even Wittgenstein could save from the fly bottle. My grandfather was eleven when his mother died, his new stepmother didn't much like him, and he left home at fourteen and spent his first night of freedom behind a pile of firewood on Hakaniemi Square. Then there was my own mother, who at the age of five was evacuated to Sweden during the war, and in the years that followed her mother tongue shifted from Finnish to Swedish and back again several times. To my surprise, a few years ago I stumbled upon the fact that around half of my father's extended family had emigrated to the

United States between 1890 and 1910, they passed the block tests at Ellis Island, and after this they quickly spread out across the continent from Massachusetts to Ironwood, Michigan, from Big Spring, Amarillo and San Mateo in the south to Portland and Alberta, Canada, in the north. One can only imagine the most commonplace reasons for emigrating, people were fleeing poverty and the threat of conscription to the Russian army. The ships set sail from Hanko, on the final night before their departure the emigres danced on the rocks by the shore, and as the ship pulled out of the harbor they sang local folksongs, sometimes even the *Internationale*, or so claimed an article I'd read.

A moment later, I follow my brother out of the restaurant and down to the shore, he takes out a cigarette, the water and the light brighten his face and the leaves of the black alders. We exchange a few uneasy words, but when I looked at him there by the shore at Uunisaari, I was suddenly reminded of the discussion about the thirty-kilometer barrier, *you hit a wall*, it's like a sudden shower of hail, your mind is filled with despair and thoughts of giving up, humans are *endurance machines*. Now that even the dream of equality has disappeared, people like Kurre become scapegoats in a society that no longer believes in anything, especially equality. My brother has never been able to express what the world feels like to him, he's barely allowed to experience what he himself feels, he too is unable to keep up with the ways of the world, he too is like Björling's poems or some random Ethiopian, completely *obegriplig*, I thought to myself. We didn't speak, but we walked down to the water's edge together, the water lapped and rippled, the sunlight glinted. If someone like Kurre were to wash up on this shore, would my brother turn his back to him, or would he push him back into the sea? An endless landslide to all Ethiopians. I tried to imagine what Kurre would have looked like in my brother's eyes, what a *tangle of fantasies* he would be, those fantasies would be full of private, *hateful landslides*, in that sense a random Ethiopian was their literal landslide, an *omnipotent landslide fantasy*. I was about to tell him about Kurre when I noticed my brother's vacant expression; he was thinking of something else. Years ago, we used to laugh and cry at the same things, together, but it's better that what is right destroys families than that families destroy what is right, and yet I still couldn't bring myself to judge my brother, whose opinions did not stem from the fact that he considered himself somehow *omnipotent*; on the contrary, he'd had his fair share of bombs and paper bombs, more than his fair share, and now we were like our ancestors a century ago, an ocean opening up between us.

When Mara arrived in Helsinki the following week, I did exactly what Herling wrote that everybody at the camp was afraid of, *that a convict will be abandoned to death and there will be no record, no memory of the end of his life.* I didn't tell Mara what the uncle had said about Kurre's heart attack or death. He was in the kind of mood that I decided it best not to tell him. He'd asked me to drive him out to Inkoo, to the old summerhouse, which was for sale. He'd written down the wrong time and arrived late, which isn't like him at all, and it meant we only had a few minutes in the house before the realtor and the potential buyers turned up. We stepped outdoors so that they could look around in peace, and Mara didn't notice or didn't care that it was a warm day, the window was wide open, and the people inside could hear everything he was saying ... *What a shit hole ... I just want to get rid of this dump, put my entire childhood and family behind me,* he said. I always felt like I was the *misslyckade ynglingen* because my parents' behavior [29] toward me was so *unfriendly,* if not downright *hostile,* which is completely unnatural ... I'm not remotely interested in whether I was trying to show Kurre the kind of motherly love I wished I'd received at home ... If you set out to find emotions that are 100% pure, you'll never find any, Mara replied, almost echoing what I had said to him on the telephone.

29 Swedish: "the failed child."

Kurre always said that leaving meant he'd lost all the people he had known throughout his entire life, said Mara, and that's why having sex was almost a compulsion for him, Kurre had explained. Incidentally, at the same basilica we had visited (Mara clarified that he meant the evening we had spent walking around the city and our visit to the basilica at Trastevere), Kurre suddenly started weeping, without any apparent reason, and afterwards he hadn't attempted to explain it in the least. Every night he wanted me to cradle him in my arms or hold his dick in my hand. Then he calmed down, his muscles relaxed, his balls dropped... Death is the most terrible thing that can befall a person, but when you watch it from the side lines, it's as though nothing is happening, Mara soon said about his mother, and I winced with guilt, I thought of Kurre and his death, and each time Mara said something-something his mother, I thought something-something Kurre, and when Mara said something-something death, I reminded myself that the news of Kurre's death was as yet unconfirmed. I reminded myself many times that everything was unclear and unconfirmed, and that's why I can't tell him about Kurre's death, he would take it as a given, so it's best that he knows nothing about it. I was worried that Mara would call Turin and the uncle would say he'd already told me everything on the phone... The window directly above us was open, and I could hear the realtor's spiel outside, she was speaking with a sense of routine, and there was nothing in her tone to suggest that Mara's ramblings had fazed her in the least.

My mother wanted to die at home, and death is easier if there's someone there to keep you company, Mara said eventually. I can't bring myself to sort another single thing here, he added. Some years ago, I'd spent many weeks sorting out my father's papers and belongings... You've resolved to go through every wardrobe individually and make dozens of phone calls and take care of the dozens of things that need to be done, yet every day you have a nagging feeling that it might be easier just to sell everything lock, stock, and barrel, but then you change your mind because you might regret it, because amid all the clutter there might be something valuable and irreplaceable... I went through this with the Kontula apartment, and later on with my uncle. I'll never forgive my relatives for not organizing their affairs while they were still alive and had the chance, said Mara. My mother always said she wanted to die at home. She said she didn't intend to become a vegetable, and she didn't. Life is about confronting the fear of darkness together. People can't see their own destructiveness; instead they see themselves as essentially bright and sunny. Even my mother considered herself a good-natured, even a sunny person, but she was neither, said Mara.

As she left, the realtor seemed overly formal, from which I assumed that Mara's words must have been perfectly audible inside the house, but the very next day Mara called me and told me with a sense of satisfaction that the summerhouse in Inkoo had been sold, furniture, firewood and all, but I still didn't tell him about Kurre's death.

The following autumn, I kept only in sporadic contact with Mara, and even then our calls were brief, but one Sunday evening in late September he called me from Rome and we spoke at great length. He was still trying to track down Kurre and dig up information about him. He'd heard about an illegal who had killed another illegal in a blind panic. I doubt it was Kurre, he said, but I could hear the terror in his voice. It's easy to imagine all the dreadful things that could have happened to him, said Mara. Even then, I couldn't bring myself to tell him that no, it wasn't Kurre. Mara continued, saying that the uncle in Turin wouldn't answer the phone, and right there and then during our phone call I resolved to tell him the truth, but I didn't, Mara was still convinced that something serious had happened because neither Kurre's friend in Rome nor Ketty, whose contact details he had hunted down, had heard anything from him. Mara did not find Kurre, but instead of Kurre he stumbled upon Affile, a small town around fifty kilo-

meters from Rome, and on the town's official website
he came across a *bombastic* biography of Graziani.
It turns out that Graziani had spent his final years
in Affile, the local officials had something to do with
Mussolini's mausoleum, and to cap it all off, now they
were building a mausoleum for Graziani too. The final testament to this country's abject brainlessness,
said Mara, and yet more proof that democracies are
prepared to abandon the aims and values for which
they once strove and even fought. Kurre wouldn't get
as much as a shallow grave, but Graziani was getting his own mausoleum... In Stockholm later on, I
looked up the Affile website and uncovered various
materials relating to the mausoleum's inauguration...
A Saturday afternoon, people gathering in Affile's
central piazza with views out across the green hill-
sides, the few trees along the edge of the square of-
fering a little shade, buildings two and three floors
high line the square, at street level there are a few
stores and in the corner of the square a bar... Two
policemen in black uniforms, a third has taken off
his jacket to reveal a blue shirt, they are chatting to
the people standing around the square. People gather
in the square, black shirts, blue armbands, most are
wearing a T-shirt and shorts, or a pair of jeans cut
off above the knee, some are in white shirts, some
carrying the Italian flag, a blue banner hangs from
the top of the flagpole. A man in his fifties, dressed

in a black shirt and trousers and a baseball cap, carries a flag with a blue background and a yellow skull
with a red rose in its teeth, another man is wearing
a faded T-shirt with three pints of beer printed on
the front, instead of the pints of beer another man
has a black scorpion on a white background, a man
of around sixty is wearing a black beret with the image of an anchor decorated with large laurels and a
crown and a sailor's shirt that looks hastily sewn together, as though his wife has dressed him up as the
captain of a torpedo ship... The free-flowing event is
hosted by the town's mayor, he is wearing a dark-grey
suit and tie. A moment later, a disparate procession
begins moving, people walking in small groups toward the park, as they call the location on the hillside around 500–600 m above the town... The crowd
is mostly men, a handful of women, most of them
overweight, and the uphill walk in thirty-degree heat
is understandably arduous, and their worn and mis-
shapen shoes don't make it any easier either... Once
the sweaty affair is finally over, the crowd disperses
across the small field in front of the mausoleum, the
town officials in the front row. To one side, there are
two wooden tables with benches around them, the
kind you usually see at rest stops on the highway.
Next to the mausoleum is an old field cannon, its barrel pointing directly at the town... Soon afterwards,
someone cuts the ribbon in front of the mausoleum.

A few blares of horns and trumpets, a drumroll, a group of locals warble in chorus, people are clearly moved... by Graziani, his face in those photographs like stone... It was an ugly thing, said Mara toward the end of our call, instead of finding out what might have happened to Kurre, I stumbled upon all this brainlessness. All real and concrete life takes places hidden away, this specifically applies to people like Kurre, and it applied to Wittgenstein too, said Mara, all real life is shoved into the background, out of sight, replaced with lies and ridiculous spectacles like this. *One of us is a vegetable, either me or the world.*

When I had a few days free at the end of October, I decided to go to Uukuniemi to get the cabin ready for the winter. On the day I was supposed to leave, there was an unexpected delay, and it was late into the afternoon by the time I finally set off. The pines and spruces standing along the motorway were dark, and the proximity of winter was apparent, tangible, the landscape waiting expectantly for the frozen yellow-green waterfalls that hang over the hewn rocks and the snow verges lining the side of the road. Long before reaching Kouvola, signs in Cyrillic began to appear, advertising *Рыба*, fish. Lights illuminated the windows of isolated houses; the air carried a faint hint of smoke. As I approached Imatra, I decided to spend the night at the old State Hotel; it was so late that it would take until morning to heat the cabin. In the hotel foyer, two Russians were admiring the Jugend-style building, which to them must have looked like a fairy-tale castle. The Russians disappeared somewhere, and the old part of the hotel, where I asked for a room, appeared all but empty. I would stay here for one night, I thought. The room was pleasant, dim, the furniture and wall paneling made of dark wood, three floors below came the steady rush of the rapids. It had been exactly four months since I'd traveled to Rome to visit Mara and ended up meeting Kurre. I pulled on the hotel's terrycloth bathrobe and walked along the corridor connecting the old part of the hotel to the new. There were no other residents in sight, only the chill on my bare feet. In the changing room, the sauna door opened and a large, stocky man stepped out. There were three men sitting in the sauna, each lost in his own thoughts, I assumed they were all Russians. In the evening I go back and forth to the sauna and swim a little in the small pool, I notice I'm the only Finn in the place; everyone else is from across the border. A man of around sixty sits in the sauna with me all evening. His features are rough, his stomach looks like a basketball trying to detach itself from the rest of his body, he sits next to the stove with a bucket of water between his legs, every few minutes throwing a ladle of water on the hot stones, he doesn't look around,

doesn't even seem to notice that there are other people here too. As I am about to leave and stand in the
corridor for a moment, he comes through the door,
raises his eyebrows a little as if to ask whether to
leave the door open for me, considerate of him, then
he turns toward the other wing of the building and
walks off. I am so tired that I can't even muster the
energy to walk to Rosso across the street for a bite
to eat, as I'd been planning, but instead head to the
hotel's own restaurant, and once a couple of diners
sitting at a table in the corner get up and leave, I am
the only customer left. The exposed wooden beams,
the Jugend arches and the chairs could be from
Ukraine or Vienna, the fireplace from Cambridge, but
I couldn't picture Kurre in this room.

The world into which we are born is a rabbit, but
at some point it spins around and turns into a duck.
Or maybe the life that we live is a rabbit and at some
point that turns into a duck. This conundrum stayed
in my mind for days, I thought about what those two
things, the rabbit and the duck, really were, at what
point another figure joins the rabbit, after which
there is no return because the rabbit, having now
transformed into a duck, can never go back to being
the same rabbit it once was, it can never return to the
simple whole again. Herling was declared a criminal,
and it was to be another half a century before he was
able to return to his homeland. There were several
moments in Kurre's life when the rabbit split into

a duck, there must have been many such moments, following one after the other like footsteps, or perhaps he migrated out of the rabbit and into the duck as he gradually, one day, one detail at a time began to disappear from the world. Time and again he tried to change the course of events, as though everyone saw his life as a cartoon duck though he believed it was still the same rabbit it had always been.

Kurre's frenzied belief in his own survival was like a dream that Herling recalled having at the camp. In this dream, he returned home, and the same dream recurred so regularly that he felt joy as evening began to fall, at the thought of having the same dream again... In this dream, reality has not yet been tarnished, the rabbit-duck's first splitting hasn't yet taken place. He, Herling, is walking home from the railway station. Though it is already dark, he can see well. At first, the dusty path running parallel to the train tracks, a small copse, then a square in the middle of which stands an abandoned villa... a stream, after that a small hill where they used to bury horses during the First World War, the pond, *their* pond, now full of reeds. Nearby, tall alders surround his house. The evening is cool but dry. The full moon has settled above the old mill, bright as a coin. From the fields come the calls of wild ducks and the splash of water. He approaches two larches standing next to each other. As a child, he imagined this was the place where two ghosts met. The old fear of ghosts returns, and he runs away. He opens the gate into the garden, carefully climbs to the ledge on top of the wall and looks inside the house, right into the dining room. Sitting around the table he sees his father, the housemaid, both his sisters, his brother with his wife and daughter. He taps the window with his fingertips. They all stand up to welcome him home after all these years, and at the same moment he awakes to his own sobs, his hands clasped against his chest. Night in the barracks surrounds him, and in another of Herling's descriptions of the barracks, one can conclude that everyone had a dream of his own, one not dissimilar from Herling's own. A symphony of sounds: initially just snoring, then whistles of breath, a doleful moaning, quiet at first, then becoming louder and growing to an incessant lament, punctuated only by the occasional spasm of dry, tearless whimpering. Someone cries out in his sleep, another sits up in bed, flailing at an invisible intruder, he looks around without seeing anything, snaps awake, then with a deep sigh slumps back into bed. As they sleep, the famished men grind their teeth, they try to suck something through their half-open lips, slurping at nothingness, the air whistles in their pouting mouths, they toss and turn from one side to the other, muttering or whimpering in their sleep. Eventually the dreamy, irregular murmur grows to an uninterrupted hymn of thanks, sung to God.

One of the men in the barracks tried to realize this shared dream.

Herling recounts an attempted escape that became the stuff of legend at the camp, and the more I read, the more the story reminded me of Kurre, forming yet another link to his life.

The man behind the escape was a Finn by the name of Rusto Karinen. Herling spelt the name oddly, I assume it must be Risto, and though events ended as they did, the mere fact of a brazen bid for freedom gave others the strength to endure from one day to the next. This story was told often, the audience knew it by heart, but still they listened with bated breath, always giving the same excited cries and asking the same questions at exactly the same spots. The only person who was relaxed was Karinen himself, lying on the upper berth and dangling his legs over the end of the bunk. Karinen had defected from Finland to the Soviet Union in 1933. He was a skilled steel worker and had adapted to his new life in Leningrad very well, but in the wave of arrests that followed Kirov's assassination Karinen ended up being sent to the gulags and wound up in Yertsevo in the summer of 1939. In winter 1940, he decided to escape. Karinen knew the border regions well; after all, he had already crossed the border illegally once before. He planned to walk by day and sleep by night in villages along the way. First he would head to the

southern shores of Lake Onega and from there to
the northern shores of Lake Ladoga. All you had to
do was keep traveling west, he said. He didn't have
a compass, only a few slices of ryebread, a knob of
butter, some vegetable oil, a few onions, three boxes
of matchsticks, some money, and on the morning of
his escape he pulled his prisoner's uniform over the
old suit he'd been wearing when he first arrived at
the camp. I became so interested in his flight that I
checked the route on the map. To the old border, it
was 450km, to the new border a further 130km, and
once the Interim Peace took effect, Karinen's escape
route would have taken him right to Uukuniemi. He
would have been wandering around the same forests
that I was to drive through the following day after
leaving Imatra, and for the final few kilometers before the new border he would have followed the same
narrow, dilapidated dirt track that split off from the
road to Uukuniemi and led to the old border post
one kilometer away that had been closed now for
several years... At points barely three meters wide,
decades ago the old dirt track used to be the main
route to Sortavala. Birch branches encroached on
the track from both sides. The ground was covered
in wood debris, some years ago the border post was
open to foresting freight, but not to private traffic; in the mid 1990s the border was opened to bus
tourism for a short while. When the logger came to

look at the fallen birches, he told me that everything changed as soon as you crossed the border, *the kind of thing you'd see in Africa...* At the border, the road ends at a barrier, in the distance you can see the now abandoned border post, its steel bollards, motion detectors and floodlights, by the road is the familiar red palm, no-man's-land, the camera tower and a sign with a picture of a camera and the text *Tekninen valvonta, Teknisk övervakning, Technical control, Техническое наблюдение.*

Karinen made his escape during the daily break while working out in the forest. He estimated that if the guards only noticed he had absconded at the end of the shift, he would have a five-hour head start. He spent the whole day trudging across crusted snow in freezing weather. As darkness fell, he heard rifle shots in the distance and concluded that they must now know that he was missing, but night would give him time, the search party wouldn't set out after him until morning. He tried to increase his head start but lost his sense of direction in the pitch dark and was forced to stop. He dug a deep hole in the snow, covered it with thick spruce branches, lit a small fire, straightened his legs around it and kept the flame burning. I thought of Kurre somewhere on the slopes of the Alps. Karinen didn't sleep at all that night, though neither did he have the sensation of being awake. He was free for the first time in five years, but he didn't feel free. He listened to the sounds of the dark forest, dozed off and woke up to his own cries as he imagined himself turning in his bed in the barracks. Several times that night he had to stand up, jump around and beat his hands against his flanks to keep himself warm. When the sun finally began to rise, he thought he could hear the barking of dogs and human voices, and prepared himself to flee deeper into the forest, but the sounds never returned. After washing his face with snow, Karinen looked at the position of the sun, deduced which way was west, and set off. Heavy clods of snow fell from the spruces, making him imagine he was being followed. He used a long stick to check the ground ahead of him for wolf traps; Kurre had said that when his uncle was walking near the border regions, he did the same thing in fear of landmines. In the forest clearings, giant spruces had been blown down in a storm. Once an hour, Karinen stops to see whether he can hear the sounds of anyone pursuing him but assumes that the dogs must have lost his scent in the powdery snow. The following night he sleeps for the first time since his escape and only wakes up the next morning. He had planned to avoid any villages for the first week, during which time he estimated he would be able to walk at least eighty kilometers. On the fourth evening, he is digging his pit in the snow when he sees a flash of light in the distance, then a searchlight sweeps across the forest and disappears all at once. He is terrified. There must be a camp nearby. He doesn't dare light a fire. He lies in his dugout, wrapped in his clothes, and raises his feet onto a spruce branch. He almost freezes to death, and the following morning it takes all his strength to haul himself upright. He sets off again, hoping to be able to walk around the camp that he concludes must be around twenty kilometers from Yertsevo. He forgets to follow the position of the sun and heads northwest, away from where he saw the searchlight. He walks slowly, stumbling and falling. He has difficulty swallowing his daily ration of bread. He rubs snow into his forehead, which feels like it is ablaze. He imagines tears running down his cheeks, though he is not crying. He talks to himself, in Finnish, and when he runs out of things to say, he recalls the songs and prayers of his childhood. As night falls, there are no lights. He starts a fire and wakes up whenever it needs more wood. Next he wakes to a curious sensation, that *he both is and is not the man that he is*. He remembers escaping the camp, yet he still imagines himself setting off with the other prisoners to their worksite in the woods. He realizes he has a fever and his body is numb. The following day, he can barely trudge onward and cannot remember which direction is which. In the afternoon he sits down by a tree and drifts into a slumber. When he wakes up, it is already night. He takes fright, cries out and imagines he can hear a reply. He runs off, collapses in the snow, then soon gets up and starts another fire. As the flames warm him, he decides that he simply must find other people, he needs to rest and gather his strength. He spends the whole of the next day walking, and in the afternoon he sees columns of smoke in the distance. That evening he crosses a clearing, behind which are the lights from a few cabins. He doesn't care to take off his prison uniform but opens the door of the nearest cabin, slumps onto a bench and loses consciousness.

After a week of trudging through the forests, the village where Karinen found himself was only thirteen kilometers from the camp at Yertsevo. The villagers took him back to the camp and handed him over to the guards. When his escape had been discovered, the guards hadn't even bothered chasing him; it was clear that he would either die in the forest or return of his own volition. Like an obedient Dubliner, Rusto (as Herling spells his Christian name) ended up back where he started, and the camp guards set about beating him without even waiting for him to regain consciousness. After this, Rusto hovered between life and death for three months, and even after that he spent a further two months in the camp's infirmary. Herling explains that Karinen always ended his story in exactly the same way: freedom isn't for us, though we are not in chains, we are chained to this place for the rest of our lives. We can escape, but in the end we always come back again. Whenever one of the prisoners tried to argue with him, saying surely it was worth it after all, a week's freedom and five months in hospital, Karinen replied just as Kurre would have replied, *when freedom itself is against us, how can we escape?*

Herling doesn't tell us what became of Karinen, he doesn't know, but statistics suggest there is a 99% chance that he never made it out alive. An unknown prisoner dies without the slightest quiver of a seismographic needle, I thought back to that afternoon at the Solfatara, the deceased and their paths. Toward the end of his life, when Wittgenstein already knew that his remaining time could be counted in months and weeks, he wrote a series of notes on certainty. However, the one thing he knew with absolute certainty is curiously absent from the text. Instead, he writes about G.E. Moore's hand gestures and the claim *I know that here is a hand*, which Mara liked so much. If someone were to say to Moore, *I do not know that here is a hand*, what might he respond? *Nothing.* Or perhaps, *take a closer look.* But if Mara wanted to believe that Kurre and people like him truly can survive, what can one say to that?

In the days between Christmas and New Year, when Mara was planning to relocate from Rome back to Helsinki, out of the blue he received a phone call from Milan. It was Kurre. He wanted to meet Mara in Rome the following day, then would return to Milan the day after and from there travel to Biella, where he still lived, and immediately asked if Mara could pay his return train fare. As soon as Kurre hung up, Mara called me in Stockholm, which I was visiting at the time. He was emotional and happy, as was I, a sense of relief spreading through my shoulders. I tried to call Kurre's uncle right away, but he didn't pick up. Mara told me that Kurre had apologized for not keeping in touch, he'd been ill. After that night in EUR, I thought Kurre was needy and vulnerable and I'd seen the way he flagrantly abused Mara's kindness, but however complex a web of abusive bonds existed between them, I'd witnessed a few sincere moments between them too, and that was enough.

The following day, Mara went to meet him at the railway station. They had agreed to eat at a restaurant, *a good restaurant*, Mara told me in advance. It was New Year's Eve, and they called me from the restaurant. Kurre sounded merry. *Kippis kaukaa,* he said, *a toast from afar.* In Biella, Kurre had been preparing for another attempt to cross the border into Switzerland, but something had happened, something for which there was still no explanation or diagnosis.

He had started to experience periods of dizziness, and at times these fits were so extreme that he couldn't stand up. This must be what his uncle had heard about, I thought. It wasn't until weeks later that Kurre had finally seen a doctor, who said he was probably suffering from benign positional vertigo or the virus-based vestibular neuritis, I heard, but in any case he had to shelve his plans to cross the border, and luckily he had a roof over his head... When the positional dizziness struck him, he staggered, slumped to his knees, sometimes in the street, once it even happened in the middle of a shopping mall, the way people stagger in unseaworthy boats, water churning around them, everyone suffering from dizziness, vomiting, pissing and shitting on one another. In EUR, Kurre had said that even a tiny ledge amid the crashing waves was enough to sustain life, now the asphalt was swaying beneath him like a two-meter surge, at his apartment the bed lurched as he lay in it, and the floor lurched as he crawled to the toilet, but if he had ended up in the hands of a gang of drunken vigilantes, as Mara had feared, not even his illness would have protected him, the gang would have treated him the same way the guards had treated the unconscious Rusto at Yertsevo... And rising up in front of him were the Alps, which he would have to cross. At that moment, the great Alpine crossings of the past, Hannibal with his war elephants, Napoleon with his Italian army, suddenly felt mundane. I chuckled out loud when I thought back to that night in EUR, as Kurre was about to go to sleep in the early hours of the morning. *I am like Napoleon; I can sleep in any circumstances...* Kurre was heading back north. He said he would try once more, give it one last shot, and if it didn't work, he didn't know what he would do. I urged him *when he leaves* to do as Wittgenstein had done outside the cabin in Skjolden when he set off to cross the fjord in a row boat during an autumn storm, and spit over his shoulder; this was the best advice I could give him. The next day, Mara called me after saying goodbye to Kurre at the railway station. The only unpleasant part of Kurre's visit was that it had felt like their final meeting, he said. Mara had given him a new shirt, the Lindeberg was in such a state that there was no point even putting it in the washing machine. Despite feeling glad that they had met up again, the phone calls left me feeling conflicted. I couldn't imagine that Kurre would actually make it, and it was all too easy to give people new shirts or advice or to pay their train fares, and I hadn't even told Mara about Kurre's death.

On Monday, I spent the afternoon at the Kungliga Biblioteket and didn't even attempt to get on with my own work, but instead began going through materials I'd found about Ethiopia. I had brought some photocopies to Stockholm with me, Björling and

Wittgenstein's handwritten papers, and I noted how their handwriting resembled that in the last message written by Lundström the driver (*hem*, home, underlined twice) when he was transported to Negele on the back of a truck with the other wounded. The handwriting of all three men made me think of the quiver of a seismographic needle, completely different from the affected, self-important hand of the Italian lieutenant colonel Nerio Brunetti in which in May 1936 he had written one of the paper bombs that Agge described. Brunetti was the air-force commander, and it was very possible that he had taken part in the bombing of Hylander's camp. When I compared their respective hands, it occurred to me that Brunetti's plane might conceivably have dropped the bomb whose shrapnel killed Lundström, and that meant I was comparing the handwriting of both killer and victim. In the evening, still pondering these questions on the train to Arlanda airport, I recalled that Agge had mentioned crossing the River Awash, the same river that Kurre had mentioned that night in EUR, the river on whose banks Lucy had been discovered. Agge mentions that he briefly *bathed* in the river, it was in the same region as another river that it had proved very tough to cross. At seven-thirty in the evening, as I was sitting in Arlanda's Terminal 5 waiting for my Norwegian flight back to Helsinki, my attention was drawn to the crew of an Ethiopian

Airlines flight as they walked through security, all of
them in dark-green uniforms, a woman walked in
front of me, effortlessly pushing a trolley with her
bags, her skin like Kurre's. The group waited for a
moment until the Swedish airport official turned,
then with almost peeved impatience released the
blue belt from between two metal posts and let the
Ethiopians through, and it was only then that I realized Kurre really would make one last go of it.

In May, two weeks after Finland's *landslide* election,
Mara received a postcard that had been redirected
from his former apartment in Rome. It was post-
marked in Klagenfurt and read simply *I did it*, and
beneath that, *K*. Mara hadn't the faintest idea how
Kurre had ended up in Klagenfurt, just across the
Italian border in Austria. He never worked out what
Kurre was doing in Klagenfurt, was he just visiting,
did he live there now, had he managed to sort his life
out or was he in another *Somali house*, in this respect
I did it remained something of an enigma, as Mara put
it… I hadn't heard from my brother since the episode
at Uunisaari, but I felt I should tell him about this *I
did it*, by way of encouragement, for him, as though
my gently clenched fist had again pressed against his
chest, no matter how great an ocean had opened up
between us that boats of refugees simply could not
cross. My Herling piece never progressed, but even

in its unfinished state it formed a link back to the Ethiopian, though neither I nor Mara know anything at all about his life. Mara even said that Kurre may in fact have already registered himself in Italy, hence all the talk of Sweden and Switzerland. Kurre and everything about his brittle life, scurrying here and there like so many ants along their pathways, was a meandering response to my brother's straight and narrow path, his *big deal*, and though perhaps there are no real facts about Kurre's life, the links leading to the cusp of his life are real, unlike the landslide fantasies about Kurre and all those like him. Tired of omniscience, both in the world and its stories (*big deal*), I prefer to follow the example of the ants, I even stumbled upon the fact that they mark their paths with a chemical trace, emitting a pheromone that other ants can recognize, and an amount of that pheromone no bigger than a printed dot on the page is enough for one ant to follow another ant to the ends of the earth.

I was in the countryside when Mara called. It felt as though the walk that had started eleven months earlier in front of Carbonara at six o'clock on Midsummer's Eve was finally nearing its conclusion, and when later that night we left Villa Lante at two or three in the morning and walked down Gianicolo laughing at what so-and-so had said, Mara was full of laughter, the trees were fragrant, the air warm and soft, and on the grass next to the pavement, spaced a few meters apart, stood the busts of Garibaldi's soldiers, among them was a Finn, said Mara, though he didn't know where. This place was the site of a battle in the mid 19th century, hence all the busts. There were plenty of busts along the edge of the lawn, dozens if not hundreds, probably a thousand, said Mara. People can adapt to anything, he laughed as we crossed the piazza. I wasn't sure whether he meant the evening at Lante or everything, the ways of the world. Here in Rome you can't go for a walk in the forest, he said. There are no forests here, and if there were you wouldn't be able to walk around in them, they would turn into dumping grounds and you'd probably get mugged. Amused, he started going through what so-and-so had said and what he thought about endurance runners. Around him were row upon row of sycamores, their trunks variegated like camouflage, ancient trees that had seen first the people themselves, then the busts erected in their honor. Bullets were embedded deep in their trunks, as is common with trees at battlegrounds, but in their boughs there were infinite numbers of branches and dark, three-lobed leaves full of life. This is almost like being in the forest, I told Mara, but he was laughing and not really listening. The hillside leading down toward the city was overgrown with bushes, further down there were different deciduous and coniferous trees, even a small cluster of bamboo, I recall.

Around us was the sound of insects; even at this hour it was unfathomably warm. Mara was still talking about the busts we had just walked past, and the one Finn among their number. All statues are built to commemorate a battle or massacre or some other kind of horseplay, he said. After this, he laughed, said something ironic, and at that moment I assumed he was laughing at our evening or the Finns at Lante, *write it*, he said but didn't tell me quite what he meant by that, perhaps my Herling piece, then he made something up, joking or half-joking, and I didn't know whether it was intended to be written on busts that were yet to be erected, whether it was from a book, whether I should write it down, or whether this was supposed to be the last word on some subject or other. At the time, I imagined it must have been ironic, must have had something to do with our evening at Lante, but thinking about it now, whatever it was, it wasn't ironic, not at all, and when I think about everything that happened soon afterwards, those words are full of gratitude and acceptance, soon afterwards we were drinking with the Ethiopian, laughing through the night in an apartment in EUR, laughing and drinking, and now Mara's phrase invokes laughter and merriment and this unknown man, and he too deserves some kind of statue. I don't know where Mara came up with the phrase, whether he'd heard it somewhere else. When we reached the bottom of Gianicolo, he said he was going off to find *the Ethiopian*. We said our goodbyes, and half an hour later, before going to sleep, I wrote his words down.

I have erected this statue in order to laugh.

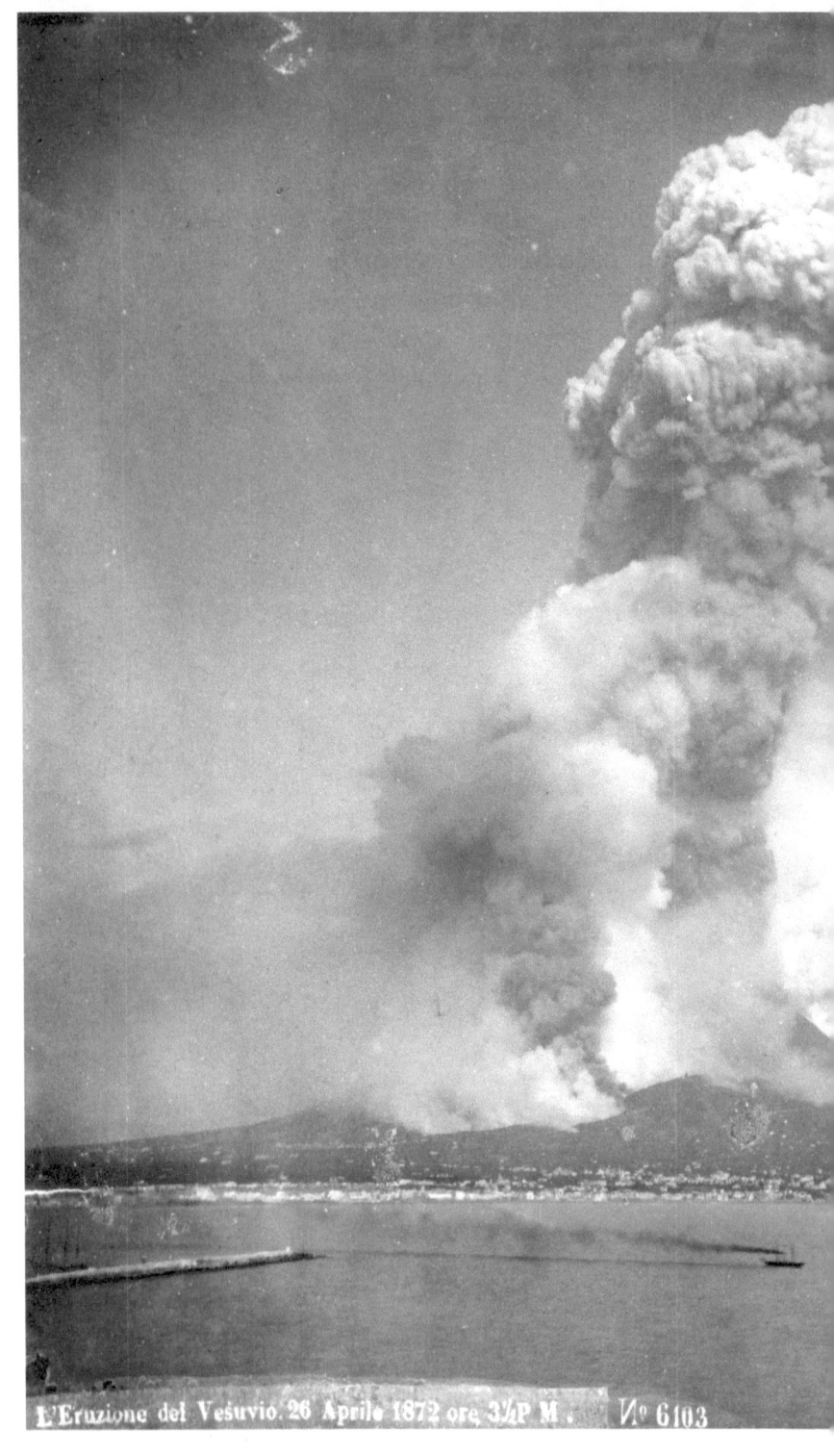

L'Eruzione del Vesuvio. 26 Aprile 1872 ore 3½P M. № 6103

To refresh my memory, I have used two biographies of Ludwig Wittgenstein: Brian McGuinness's *Wittgenstein: A Life. Young Ludwig, 1889–1921* (Duckworth, 1988) and Ray Monk's *Ludwig Wittgenstein. The Duty of Genius* (Vintage, 1991), as well as James C. Klagge's *Wittgenstein in Exile* (The MIT Press, 2011), which sketches important aspects of Wittgenstein's work in relation to his own life. Of Wittgenstein's own works, my central sources are *Notebooks 1914–1916*, eds G.H. von Wright and G.E.M. Anscombe (Basil Blackwell, 1961), *Tractatus-Logico-Philosophicus*, eds C.K. Ogden and F.P. Ramsey (Kegan Paula, Trench, Trubner & Co., 1922) and *Philosophical Investigations*, tr. G.E.M. Anscombe (Basil Blackwell, 1958).

This work contains quotations from the works of the Polish writer Gustaw Herling-Grudziński, notably *A World Apart*, tr. Joseph Marek / Andrzej Ciołkosz (Roy Publishers, 1951); *Volcano and Miracle: A Selection from the Journal Written at Night*, tr. Ronald Strom (Viking, 1996); and Herling's story 'The Tower' from the collection *The Island: Three Tales*, tr. Ronald Strom (Peter Owen, 1990).

Throughout the section of this book following Gunnar Agge and the expedition of the Swedish Red Cross in Abyssinia, my main sources are Gunnar Agge's *Med röda korset i fält: minnen och intryck från svenska abessinienambulansen 1935–1936* (In the field with the Red Cross: memories and impressions from a Swedish ambulance in Abyssinia 1935–1936; Albert Bonniers Förlag, Stockholm, 1936); Fride Hylander's *I detta tecken: med svenska Röda Korset i Abessinien* (Under this sign: with the Swedish Red Cross in Abyssinia; Evangeliska

Fosterlands-Stiftelsens Bokförlag, Stockholm, 1936); and Heli von Rosen's *Dödsorsak Ogaden. Om flyg och politik med Carl Gustaf von Rosen i Afrika* (Cause of death: Ogaden. On flight and politics in Africa with Carl Gustaf von Rosen; Atlantis, 2013). In addition to these works, I have tried to read all available material written by those who took part in the Finnish and Swedish Red Cross expeditions to Abyssinia (including the works of Håkan Mörne and Knut Johansson) as well as Swedish and Italian materials about the expeditions and the natural environment in the region.

Drawing on contemporary materials, Carl-Johan Malmberg has written about the catastrophe that ensued from the bombing of poet Gunnar Björling's house in 'Hus störtat in. Du, bygg det förnyades hand! Gunnar Björling och katastrofen' ('House collapsed. You, build the replenished one's hand!' Gunnar Björling and the catastrophe'; Lyrikvännen 1993: 5). Erik Gamby has also drawn on this material in an unpublished manuscript. Fredrik Hertzberg has recently published a biography of Björling, and here the bombing is explored in great depth: *"Mitt språk är ej i orden." Gunnar Björlings liv och verk* ("My language is not in the words." Gunnar Björling's life and works; SLS/Appell Förlag, 2018). The first I heard about this episode was from an old friend to whom, in the early 1950s, Björling had recounted the events directly after the bombing and to whom he had shown the scraps of charred, shrunken papers that he called his ashen archive.

Image on pages 253–54:

L'Eruzione del Vesuvio. Giorgio Sommer, 3.30 P.M., April 26, 1872.

COLOPHON

ONE THOUSAND AND ONE
was handset in InDesign CC.

The text & display font is *Adobe Warnock*.

Book design & typesetting: Alessandro Segalini

Cover design: CMP

ONE THOUSAND AND ONE
is published by Contra Mundum Press.

Contra Mundum Press   New York · London · Melbourne

CONTRA MUNDUM PRESS

Dedicated to the value & the indispensable importance of the individual voice, to works that test the boundaries of thought & experience.

The primary aim of Contra Mundum is to publish translations of writers who in their use of form and style are *à rebours*, or who deviate significantly from more programmatic & spurious forms of experimentation. Such writing attests to the volatile nature of modernism. Our preference is for works that have not yet been translated into English, are out of print, or are poorly translated, for writers whose thinking & æsthetics are in opposition to timely or mainstream currents of thought, value systems, or moralities. We also reprint obscure and out-of-print works we consider significant but which have been forgotten, neglected, or overshadowed.

There are many works of fundamental significance to *Weltliteratur* (& *Weltkultur*) that still remain in relative oblivion, works that alter and disrupt standard circuits of thought — these warrant being encountered by the world at large. It is our aim to render them more visible.

For the complete list of forthcoming publications, please visit our website. To be added to our mailing list, send your name and email address to: info@contramundum.net

Contra Mundum Press
P.O. Box 1326
New York, NY 10276
USA

2012   *Gilgamesh*
        Ghérasim Luca, *Self-Shadowing Prey*
        Rainer J. Hanshe, *The Abdication*
        Walter Jackson Bate, *Negative Capability*
        Miklós Szentkuthy, *Marginalia on Casanova*
        Fernando Pessoa, *Philosophical Essays*
2013   Elio Petri, *Writings on Cinema & Life*
        Friedrich Nietzsche, *The Greek Music Drama*
        Richard Foreman, *Plays with Films*
        Louis-Auguste Blanqui, *Eternity by the Stars*
        Miklós Szentkuthy, *Towards the One & Only Metaphor*
        Josef Winkler, *When the Time Comes*
2014   William Wordsworth, *Fragments*
        Josef Winkler, *Natura Morta*
        Fernando Pessoa, *The Transformation Book*
        Emilio Villa, *The Selected Poetry of Emilio Villa*
        Robert Kelly, *A Voice Full of Cities*
        Pier Paolo Pasolini, *The Divine Mimesis*
        Miklós Szentkuthy, *Prae, Vol. 1*
2015   Federico Fellini, *Making a Film*
        Robert Musil, *Thought Flights*
        Sándor Tar, *Our Street*
        Lorand Gaspar, *Earth Absolute*
        Josef Winkler, *The Graveyard of Bitter Oranges*
        Ferit Edgü, *Noone*
        Jean-Jacques Rousseau, *Narcissus*
        Ahmad Shamlu, *Born Upon the Dark Spear*
2016   Jean-Luc Godard, *Phrases*
        Otto Dix, *Letters, Vol. 1*
        Maura Del Serra, *Ladder of Oaths*
        Pierre Senges, *The Major Refutation*
        Charles Baudelaire, *My Heart Laid Bare & Other Texts*

SOME FORTHCOMING TITLES

AGRODOLCE SERIES

2020   Dejan Lukić, *The Oyster*
2022   Ugo Tognazzi, *The Injester*

HYPERION
On the Future of Æsthetics   2006–2023

To read samples and order current & back issues of *Hyperion*,
visit contramundumpress.com/hyperion
Edited by Rainer J. Hanshe & Erika Mihálycsa (2014 ~)

 **CONTRA MUNDUM PRESS**

is published by Rainer J. Hanshe
Typography & Design: Alessandro Segalini
Publicity & Marketing: Alexandra Gold

THE FUTURE OF KULCHUR
A PATRONAGE PROJECT

With bookstores and presses around the world struggling to survive, and many actually closing, we are forming this patronage project as a means for establishing a continuous & stable foundation to safeguard our longevity. Through this patronage project we would be able to remain free of having to rely upon government support &/or other official funding bodies, not to speak of their timelines & impositions. It would also free CMP from suffering the vagaries of the publishing industry, as well as the risk of submitting to commercial pressures in order to persist, thereby potentially compromising the integrity of our catalog.

CAN YOU SACRIFICE $10 A WEEK FOR KULCHUR?

For the equivalent of merely 2–3 coffees a week, you can help sustain CMP and contribute to the future of kulchur. To participate in our patronage program we are asking individuals to donate $500 per year, which amounts to $42/month, or $10/week. Larger donations are of course welcome and beneficial. All donations are tax-deductible through our fiscal sponsor Fractured Atlas. If preferred, donations can be made in two installments. We are seeking a minimum of 300 patrons per year and would like for them to commit to giving the above amount for a period of three years.

Part tax-deductible donation, part exchange, for your contribution you will receive every CMP book published during the patronage period as well as 20 books from our back catalog. When possible, signed or limited editions of books will be offered as well.

WHAT WILL CMP DO WITH YOUR CONTRIBUTIONS?

Your contribution will help with basic general operating expenses, yearly production expenses (book printing, warehouse & catalog fees, etc.), advertising and outreach, and editorial, proofreading, translation, typography, design and copyright fees. Funds may also be used for participating in book fairs and staging events. Additionally, we hope to rebuild the *Hyperion* section of the website in order to modernize it.

From Pericles to Mæcenas & the Renaissance patrons, it is the magnanimity of such individuals that have helped the arts to flourish. Be a part of helping your kulchur flourish; be a part of history.

HOW

To lend your support & become a patron, please visit the subscription page of our website: contramundum.net/subscription

For any questions, write us at: info@contramundum.net